The Cat Next Door

Also by Marian Babson

The Cat Next Door

Marian Babson

THOMAS DUNNE BOOKS
St. Martin's Minotaur
New York

THOMAS DUNNE BOOKS.
An imprint of St. Martin's Press.

www.minotaurbooks.com

ISBN 0-312-20925-8

First published in Great Britain under the title
Deadly Deceit by Constable, an imprint of
Constable & Robinson Ltd

First U.S. Edition: April 2002

10 9 8 7 6 5 4 3 2 1

To Mary Ellis Lebert

in loving memory

Chapter One

'Who says we're a dysfunctional family?' Margot looked around the dinner table. 'We all came back for the trial, didn't we?'

No one looked up. Heads bowed, completely absorbed in the contents of their plates, they all let the silence lengthen.

'I'm still not sure that was such a good idea.' Aunt Emmeline met her eyes briefly in the dead-level stare that had quelled a thousand boisterous schoolgirls. 'Everyone gathering, that is. It could look . . . valedictory.'

'Not at all. Showing solidarity, that's what it is.' The words seemed to be wrenched from Cousin Henry, almost against his will. He appeared to regret them immediately, darting a quick guilty look at Aunt Millicent.

But Millicent Morton was serenely oblivious. She neatly cut a small square from her slice of roast beef and piled it on the side of her plate alongside all the other neat squares of beef. Occasionally, very occasionally, she actually ate one. But not very often and not very many. No one might have spoken; no one else might have been sitting at the table with her. A book waited, face down, beside her plate and her hand hovered over it sporadically before she seemed to recall the proprieties and withdrew it. Her gaze lingered wistfully on the print of the back cover which detailed the delights awaiting within. It was clear that all she wanted to do was to escape with her book and continue reading.

Henry had incautiously neglected to return his attention to his plate immediately. Margot caught his eye and lifted her eyebrows at him.

He lifted his shoulders in reply; in fuller explanation, he also lifted his hands briefly, palms upward, before returning his full attention to his plate. The moment of communication was over.

Margot glanced around the table again. If any of them had noticed the byplay, they were not revealing it. Never had a dinner received such absorbed attention, yet Margot would have been prepared to bet that no one could say what they had been eating if the plates were to be suddenly whipped away from them. No compliments to the chef on this one.

The only sounds were the clink of cutlery against china and the jangle of Aunt Christabel's charm bracelet as she sawed at what must have been a tough corner of beef. What would they do when they had finished their meal and had no escape from facing each other and trying to make conversation?

'If you're not going to eat that –' Uncle Wilfred had finished and was spurred to movement. He leaned over and speared a forkful of neglected meat from his wife's plate. 'Then I'll eat it!'

'Why not?' Aunt Emmeline muttered. 'You usually do.'

Uncle Wilfred was the one who had changed most during the traumatic eighteen months since Margot had last seen him. The buttons of his shirt strained at the buttonholes and a thick rim of flesh bulged above his collar; he must have put on at least thirty pounds. If he'd been eating Aunt Millicent's meals as well as his own, no wonder.

The strain showed on all of them in different ways, but the most obvious was the paler skins and the tiny lines around eyes and mouths, surely more wrinkles

8

than would have accrued in a normal eighteen-month period. There was also a common tendency to turn a head abruptly and appear to be listening for something.

Yet it hadn't been eighteen months, Margot reminded herself, that was just the length of time she had been away. Not so terribly long, really, and yet so much had happened to all of them in that length of time – herself included. If she had returned a year ago, happy and flourishing herself, she would have found everything bright and pleasant and just the way she always remembered it . . . remembered them. It was less than a year ago that the abyss had opened up at their feet.

Their world had changed overnight, plunging them into a nightmare that would never really end. Shock waves had engulfed them all, the undertow had dragged them down, choking, gasping and bewildered, into depths they could never have imagined. The unthinkable, the unbelievable, the irrevocable, had happened to them, had invaded their private lives, their home. Even after the trial, after the verdict – whatever it might be – life would never be the same again.

That was the truth of murder.

The big mahogany dining-table had been rearranged to mask the missing places. It was smaller than usual at a family reunion; one, or possibly two, of the leaves had not been used. The seating was wider spaced. Even so, it still seemed too large. Of course, there were still a few more members of the family to come.

'Where's Richard?' Margot asked softly. 'I thought I'd have seen him before this.'

'Richard is staying in town, holding the fort at the office. Uncle Wilfred is too . . . distracted . . . to handle everything right now – he's concentrating on the defence while Richard tends to the business.'

'Good old Richard,' Margot said, 'a tower of strength, as usual.' Was it a comfort to Wilfred and Millicent that their eldest child had turned out so well, or did it simply point up their failure with his siblings?

'He's collecting Justin and Fenella at Heathrow right now,' Henry said. 'They'll be along soon.'

'Shouldn't they be here by now?' Christa's charm bracelet tinkled as she turned it, seeking the tiny fob watch which always seemed to get lost among the mementoes of past triumphs. 'Do you think their plane was late . . . or something?'

A ripple of unease swept over them. Nothing could be trusted any more, nothing could be depended upon.

'Steady on,' Henry said. 'If the plane had crashed, we'd have heard about it by now.' He dabbed abstractedly at one corner of his mouth with his napkin and pushed back his chair. 'Perhaps we should check the half-hour news bulletin on the radio. There might be a power failure at Heathrow . . . or something.'

Christa's bracelet jangled an alarm as she tugged at the scarf around her neck, then loosened it, then took it off completely and retied it. Then she seemed at a loss as to what to do next. There was another jangle from her bracelet as she twisted it to consult her watch charm again.

Emmeline's lips tightened. Wilfred continued to eat from his wife's plate. Millicent did not appear to notice; her hand rested lightly on her book and she seemed to be reading, with great interest, the name and address of the publisher.

'It's all right, there's nothing on the news.' Nanny Helston had obviously been monitoring from the serving hatch. She came into the room and began collecting empty plates briskly. 'Stay where you are. It's raspberry fool for pudding.'

'Good, good,' Wilfred responded heartily. Even the others relaxed a bit. Raspberry fool had always been a favourite and there'd be ratafia biscuits with it, too. Once that would have been taken as surety that God was in His heaven and all was right with the world.

Now it simply meant that even Nanny was striving desperately to try to make the world seem normal.

Especially Nanny, who must be fighting her own demons. She had brought up all of the younger members of the family, sliding effortlessly from position to position when they no longer needed a nanny, but Aunt Milly was frantic for a housekeeper. Without a family of her own, Nanny was content to remain in her comfortable quarters, with her own television, car and the additional help of an occasional cook and au pair.

'No au pair in residence?' Margot asked. That was another of the missing faces around the table. The others didn't bear thinking about.

'Not at the moment,' Nanny said. 'We had a Swiss girl, but she was getting a bit homesick. With everything the way it is, we thought it best to let her go back to her family.'

'Encouraged her, in fact,' Henry said.

'We felt it best not to have strangers around at a time like this,' Emmeline said. 'Pleasant though she was.'

'Chink in the armour,' Wilfred grunted. 'Weak link in the chain. Media wave their chequebooks and someone like that –' He folded his jaws over the last morsel from Milly's plate and chewed savagely.

'We *did* have that problem . . . before.' Emmeline's gaze strayed to her sister, but Milly gave no indication of having heard a word. 'It was quite . . . awkward.'

'Not laying ourselves open to that again,' Wilfred said.

Emmeline shook her head forcefully. 'No, it simply wouldn't do.'

'They say there's no such thing as bad publicity, so long as they spell your name right.' Christa lifted her head and stared into Margot's eyes. 'That isn't true. Every damned bloody lie they write is put into a file with your name on it somewhere – and every time someone pulls out that file to research you, all the misquotations, the misunderstandings – the lies – are

11

there for everyone to see and repeat. All those lies will follow you around for the rest of your life, appearing in every biographical note, every interview, until they finally show up in your obituary –' She broke off in consternation, casting a guilty look at her sister.

Aunt Millicent still hadn't taken in one word anyone had said. She smiled vaguely as Nanny returned with the tray of desserts and began setting them out around the table.

'Thanks, Nan.' Margot flashed her a quick smile and, in return, felt a brief gentle tug at a lock of hair at the back of her head. That had always been Nanny's way of expressing affection . . . or warning.

Everyone had gone silent again. When Margot closed her eyes, she could still hear the whine of the jets and feel the vibration of the plane. Jet-lagged and exhausted, she had arrived only a short time ago and had not even unpacked yet. *No! Don't think about unpacking!*

Wildly, she cast about for distraction, for a safe subject to talk about. What subject was safe in a world gone mad?

'Where's Tikki?' The cat was the only one she felt able to ask about. All other absences were too poignant.

'That damned beast!' Uncle Wilfred was roused to fury.

Henry shot her a quick *Now you've done it!* look and buried himself in his raspberry fool.

'Actually, dear,' Nan said delicately, 'I'm afraid Tikki doesn't live here any more.'

'No,' Wilfred snorted. 'He only drops in now and again for a meal.'

'That's how dysfunctional we are,' Henry muttered to Margot. 'Even the cat walked out on us.'

'Tickety-boo?' Even as she said it, Margot heard how ridiculous she sounded. As though there might be another cat with a similar name they could be talking about. She had a vague fond memory of a rollicking little Abyssinian kitten with a registered name and pedi-

12

gree longer than it was. The kitten had adored them all and been adored in return.

'Gone,' Wilfred confirmed grimly. 'Jumped ship. Deserted us. Buggered off, the little bugger!'

'It wasn't his fault!' Aunt Milly suddenly flared into life. 'When Olive Stacey went on that all-fish diet, poor Tikki was just tempted beyond his strength!'

'The diet only lasted two weeks,' Uncle Wilfred snarled. 'And Olive gave up after eight days – but the cat hasn't come back yet. Ungrateful little brute!'

'Poor Olive is terribly embarrassed about it,' Milly explained to Margot. 'At first, she kept bringing him back. She must have carried him home a dozen times but, as soon as his paws hit the carpet, he was off and back at her house before she got there. Finally, it seemed better to let him stay with her, since she was willing. At least we knew where he was and that he was safe and well.'

Uncle Wilfred snorted again.

'You can't tie a cat down,' Aunt Milly insisted. 'A cat is a free spirit.'

'Free?' Wilfred's voice rose to a muted roar. 'I paid five hundred pounds for that miserable beast – and then he walked out on us!'

Clearly an animal with no sense of fiscal responsibility. For a moment, everything was the way it used to be and Margot relaxed. Dear Fred and Milly squabbling more or less amiably over something that was fairly important but not exactly world-shattering, locked in an argument neither of them could win, but determined to keep it going, drawing in other members of the family for a good old-fashioned free-for-all.

'Olive isn't getting the registration papers, though,' Wilfred continued, with a trace of malice. 'She'll never be able to show him.'

'I still think that's rather petty.' Emmeline entered the fray.

'She wouldn't want to show him – and he wouldn't

want to be shown!' Milly threw back her head and glared at Wilfred. 'He's a pet!'

'Too bad he's not *our* pet. We paid for him!' Uncle Wilfred was quivering with indignation. 'At least, I did!'

'Fred . . . Milly . . .' As usual, Nan tried to be peace-maker. 'It's probably just a passing phase. Tikki will come back –'

'Yes, when he smells something cooking that he fancies.' Wilfred would not be placated. 'He'll stroll in, eat everything you're fool enough to give him – then turn around and go back to Olive again. He always does.'

'Not always,' Milly corrected. 'Sometimes he stays around for several hours. He has a little nap and visits everyone.'

'How kind of him! How condescending! Just what I bargained for when I bought him. A visiting cat! A two-timing little –'

A bell rang in the distance. There was an abrupt silence. Everyone froze, then Wilfred slowly deflated. Aunt Milly looked around blankly, the animation died out of her face, the vague sweet smile was back. She stretched a hand towards her book and, this time, picked it up, clasping it to her like a shield.

Christa's bracelet jangled as she reached for her wine glass and drained it. Henry looked at Margot.

The bell sounded again. It was a handbell, rung expertly as by a town crier, managing to give out a sound that was both plaintive and imperative. It was going to keep on ringing until someone answered.

'You haven't seen Lynette yet, have you?' Henry asked.

14

Chapter Two

'No.' Margot shook her head. That was one of the absences she had not felt able to ask about. 'How . . . how is she?'

The bell pealed again, signalling annoyance – and, perhaps, growing panic.

'She's heard all the talking,' Christa said. 'She's afraid she's missing something. She wants to know what's going on.'

'Then why doesn't she come downstairs and find out?' What Margot considered a perfectly reasonable question was met with an awkward silence.

'You haven't seen her yet.' Emmeline pushed back her chair. 'You might as well get it over with now. We'll have no peace until you do.'

The others nodded agreement with varying degrees of uneasiness.

'Come along –' Emmeline stood in the doorway, waiting impatiently. 'Come along. She's upstairs in her –'

There was a low growling sound deep in Uncle Wilfred's throat.

'She's in the master bedroom,' Emmeline amended hastily. 'Come along!' She turned and almost fled from the room.

Margot followed more slowly, uneasily aware of some sort of warning signal still flickering in Wilfred's eyes. Aunt Milly had opened her book and was reading avidly. Henry and Christabel were too intent on their

15

raspberry fool to look up and meet any other eyes. Nan had disappeared. The bell kept ringing.

'Coming . . .' Emmeline called out. 'All *right*, Lynette, we're coming. Don't be so impatient!' She hurried up the stairs and paused before the open door, waiting for Margot to catch up.

'Who's there?' The thin voice crackled with sudden panic. 'Who's out there?'

Emmeline closed her eyes briefly and her lips tightened before she forced them into a calming smile. She motioned to Margot to follow and advanced into the room.

'Now, Lynette, I told you we were coming, you heard us climbing the stairs. Who else could it be?' If the sweet reasonableness of Emmeline's tone was a trifle strained, the child did not appear to realise it.

'Oh, yes.' There was a fragile welcoming smile to greet them. 'Hello, Cousin Margot. Did you have a good flight over?'

'I've had worse.' Margot stooped to kiss the pale cheek, slightly puzzled. Lynette was sitting up in bed, looking perfectly healthy, with no trace of a fever or a cold. Why wasn't she dressed and downstairs with the rest of the family? 'What about you? Aren't you feeling well?'

'No. I'm not well.' Lynette turned her head away. 'I feel very, very poorly.'

There was a tray on the bedside table. From the look of the empty plates, there was nothing wrong with Lynette's appetite, at any rate. Another table, on the far side of the king-sized bed, was piled with games and hobby equipment: beadwork, embroidery, petit-point, a painting set and drawing tablet, everything the bedridden invalid might desire. Behind the piled-up pillows propping her up, the shelves that formed the bedhead held books, a transistor radio, the TV remote control, a couple of fluffy animals, comfort toys not quite out-

16

grown. Everything well within reach without Lynette having to leave the bed.

Was there something wrong with her legs?

Emmeline was not meeting any questioning eyes. She busied herself with stacking the dishes on the tray into a neat little pile, then carried the tray across the room to set it down beside the door leading into the hall. At the other end of the room, another door stood ajar, opening into the en-suite bathroom.

'Now then.' Emmeline briskly pulled a book and exercise notebook from the shelf immediately behind Lynette. 'Have you finished your English assignment?'

'Almost.' Lynette twitched defensively. 'I was going to, but . . .' Her eyes closed and she leaned back against the pillows. 'I was too tired.'

Tired, yes, tired. Margot fought back a yawn. *Aren't we all?*

Margot looked again at the hobby table and saw that the embroidery ring held a pattern with just a few flowers filled in, the tapestry in its frame was only two inches wide, a band of beadwork curled despondently on top of tubes of loose beads in a plastic bag, a threaded needle was jabbed into what was intended to be a petit-point cushion cover, pieces of a jigsaw puzzle were in a tumbled heap beside a few fitted-together sections of a cuddly-pets domestic scene.

Everything started and nothing completed.

She noticed, too, a small cluster of sports books and political biographies flanking the school books and novels on the bookshelves. Uncle Wilfred was maintaining a foothold in the quarters that had belonged to him and Aunt Milly. His attitude was now explained, although it looked as though there was scant chance of his reclaiming the master suite at any time in the immediate future.

'Isn't Fenella here yet?' There was a querulous, faintly accusing note in her tone, as though it were someone's fault that Fenella hadn't arrived yet.

'She'll be here soon. But you've got Margot right now. Why don't you have a nice visit with her, while I –'

'Fenella is going to bring me a present from Tokyo.' Lynette eyed Margot speculatively. 'Did you –?'

'Lynette!' Emmeline called her to order sharply. 'Where are your manners?'

'I'm tired, so tired . . .' Lynette retreated into invalidism. She gave Margot a wan smile. 'Tomorrow,' she said. 'Tomorrow you must tell me all about New York. Tonight I'm only strong enough just to say hello to everyone.' She lay back on the pillows and closed her eyes firmly.

'Tomorrow . . .' Margot agreed, grateful for the reprieve and following Emmeline from the room. This was not the Lynette she had known. This Lynette was looking and sounding like a child but . . .

'Isn't Lynette into her teens now?' she asked.

'There has been a bit of regression, yes.' Emmeline answered the thought behind the question. 'It's something we may have to deal with . . . eventually. If it doesn't right itself naturally. But not until this is . . . over.' Her voice wavered suddenly. She turned her back on Margot abruptly and marched down the hallway and into a room at the far end, the door of which closed behind her with a firm decisive click – not actually slammed, but making it quite clear that the conversation had ended.

A *bit* of regression! Margot did a swift calculation. Lynette must be fourteen now – and she was behaving like an eight-year-old. Ten, at the most. And hadn't Lynette been heading towards being the sporty type? Margot distinctly remembered watching her on a tennis court, playing an aggressive but good-humoured game with one of the cousins. And winning school prizes for swimming and running. Claudia had always boasted that she was rearing a future Olympics winner – in one field or another.

Claudia . . .

Her eyes blurred with sudden tears, Margot stumbled and caught at the banister just in time, leaning heavily on it as she descended the stairs. She reached the foot of the stairs before she realised it and stretched out a hand blindly for balance.

Only to feel it grasped firmly and reassuringly. Henry had been waiting there for her. She opened her eyes and smiled weakly at him.

'Hooray Henry . . .' She greeted him by the old nickname.

'Not any more,' he said ruefully, squeezing her hand and releasing it. 'There's not much to hooray about these days.'

'No . . .' She slipped her hand into the crook of his arm and they strolled into the library. 'There isn't, is there?'

'You've seen Lynette?'

'How long has she been like that?'

'Ever since she . . .' He turned away and busied himself with the coffee pot and cups waiting on the long table. 'Ever since . . . Cream and sugar?'

'No sugar, thanks.' She sank into one of the button-back leather armchairs flanking the fire. The tray beside the coffee pot held a full complement of cups and saucers. She wondered how long it would be before the others appeared for their coffee. This was the first chance she had had to talk to anyone privately since she arrived late this afternoon. Might as well make the most of it.

'Will she ever be able to walk again?'

'What?' In the act of bending over to hand her coffee to her, Henry straightened up abruptly, snatching the cup away. 'Who? What are you talking about?'

'Lynette. Isn't she paralysed?'

'Not a bit of it. Where did you get that idea?'

'I've just seen her. Lying there in that king-sized bed, all her games and pastimes within easy reach. She looks so pale and frail. I just assumed . . .'

'Assumptions are dangerous things. There's nothing physically wrong with Lynette. But the shock completely traumatised her.'

'Then she can walk.'

'Of course she can. She did, in the beginning. Except that she wouldn't go out into the garden.' Henry restored her cup of coffee to her and sank down in the opposite armchair. 'Then she didn't want to come downstairs. Well, there was so much commotion going on for so long, you couldn't blame her for that. Everyone was just as glad to have her tucked up safely out of the way, to be frank. Only . . .'

'Only . . .?'

'Only . . . they've let it go on for too long. She's too well dug in now and she doesn't want to leave that room any more. It's a shame they moved her in there to begin with. It's too convenient with the bathroom en-suite, she doesn't even have to walk down the hallway to the family bathroom. It's been weeks now since she left that room at all.'

'I thought Uncle Wilfred was looking a trifle strained when I went upstairs with Emmeline. I'm surprised he allowed her to take it over like that.'

'At the time, it seemed the best thing to do. Her own room overlooked the . . . the salient part of the garden. The police were swarming out there, with electric lights set up around the taped-off area and all their equipment. We couldn't let her look out and see that. She'd seen enough.' He set down his coffee cup abruptly and looked around for something stronger. 'What about a cognac or a liqueur?'

'She found them, didn't she?' The twin sisters, Claudia and Chloe, Lynette's mother and aunt. Claudia, stretched out upon the ground; Chloe, stooping over her with the bloodied knife in her hand. 'I . . . I just know what I read in the newspaper clippings you sent me. I thought someone else might write to me about it, but they didn't. Oh, they wrote, but they never mentioned . . . what happened.'

'No, they wouldn't.' Henry poured cognac into two balloon-shaped glasses and brought one to her. 'We're all still trying to come to terms with it ourselves.'

'Yes.' It must have been unbearable, still was. 'But Milly and Wilfred seem to be coping fairly well, considering . . .'

'Is that the way it looks to you?' Henry gave a sharp bark which could have been a cough or a bitter laugh.

'Well, from what I've heard, they're coping a lot better than . . .' She found she did not want to utter the name. Someone else she hardly dared enquire about.

'Kingsley?' Henry nodded. 'He came as close to a breakdown as one could possibly get without going completely over the edge. Or perhaps he did. He was devastated, he adored Claudia.'

'And she him.' Margot could attest to that. Despite fluttering every female heart in the neighbourhood – yes, hers included – the rising young politician had had eyes for no one but Claudia from the moment they first met. He could even tell her apart from Chloe – something even Aunt Milly was not always able to do in those days – and that, in turn, had helped to win her heart. A man who could not be fooled by their games was someone special indeed – someone to be held tight.

'They were so utterly devoted to each other. It was a tragedy . . .' Henry paused and seemed to consider what he had just said. 'A tragedy for all of us,' he amended. 'I don't know how we got through it. In a way, Kingsley had it easy – he disappeared into The Priory for six weeks, even though the election was looming. And he got re-elected, when so many others weren't. No one dared mention the words "sympathy vote", but that was what it was.'

'Not necessarily,' Margot defended. 'He was always one of the best politicians in his party.'

'Good old Kingsley!' Henry gave the sharp mirthless bark again. 'Always has the women on his side!'

'That isn't fair –'

'Fair? What's fair? And what does it matter, anyway? All that's important now is the trial.' He turned his head away. 'The trial. God! It's so incredible! Chloe's trial.'

'But why?' It was the question she had been asking herself since she first heard about Chloe. 'Why?'

'God knows.' Henry shrugged. 'And, presumably, Chloe. But we can't ask the One – and the other isn't talking. Literally. She hasn't said a word all the way through.'

'What do you mean?'

'Just that. Not a word. Not to the police, not to the legal beagles, not to the doctor, not to the psychiatrist and, especially, not to us. It isn't going to do her case any good. Now that the Right to Remain Silent has been abolished, it will probably do her harm. They can't force her to talk, of course, which is just as well. It's as though she's been stricken mute.'

'But surely –' Margot's throat constricted. She felt as though she had been stricken mute herself.

'Not a word. She won't utter one syllable to explain – or to defend – herself. She's cut herself off completely, refused to see any of us. Parcels we've sent are returned unopened.' Henry shook his head. 'I wonder sometimes if she's punishing herself . . . or us. And for what.'

'I didn't realise . . .' Margot closed her eyes for a moment; immediately, the deep whine intensified in her ears, the chair seemed to vibrate. Even sitting down and leaning back, she felt dizzy and exhausted. Damn!

A homecoming to this situation was enough to cope with without jet lag as well. Yet, if it weren't for the situation, would she have come home at all? Would any of them?

Henry was saying something. She opened her eyes and caught a glimpse of something moving beyond him, on the other side of the french window leading out to the garden. Something crawling along the ground through the shadows, something that looked shadowy itself and, perhaps, rusty. A breastplate, dragging along the ground, rusty – or stained with blood . . .

'The Centurion!' she gasped, suddenly transported back to childhood.

'What?' Henry whirled about, following the line of her vision. 'Oh, you had me going for a moment there.' He laughed and opened the french window.

'You want to come in, Tikki?'

Chapter Three

The proud Abyssinian sauntered into the room as though he were doing them a favour. By his lights, he probably was.

'Hello, Tikki.' Margot held out her hand and waggled her fingers. 'Remember me?'

The cat strolled over and indulged in a good sniffing session. He seemed fascinated and Margot wondered how many unfamiliar and exotic scents were clinging to her. From her fingertips, Tikki moved on to the hem of her skirt and then to her shoes. Could he identify the smell of a foreign country, crowded airports, aviation fuel . . . loathing, misery and fear?

'I hadn't thought of the Centurion in years,' Henry said with relish. 'Zeus! How that takes me back!' His laughter invited her to join in.

Tikki gathered himself together and sprang into her lap. Whatever messages he had read from her skin and clothing, she had passed muster. He settled down in her lap.

Automatically, she stroked the soft sand-coloured fur. Not rusty, not bloodied, just sandy, evolved to act as natural camouflage in the sandy wastes of the deserts his ancestors had patrolled. He arched his neck under her soothing fingers and began purring.

'I went back, too.' She smiled reminiscently. They had invented the Centurion between them, she and Henry. As children, it had seemed so unfair that, here in St Albans, with its long centuries of history and human habitation, there had been so little trace of it all in their immediate area.

It had seemed only proper to redress this omission of history by inventing their own ghost: the Centurion from one of the Roman legions that had occupied St Albans or, as it was then known, Verulamium. He could have existed, their fertile imaginations insisted, and, from that, it was but a short step to having his ghost inhabit their garden on dark and moonless nights. What imaginations! And no wonder, surrounded as they were with Roman ruins, in an area where any garden spade might turn up ancient coins, shards of amphorae, mosaic tiles, statuettes of gods and goddesses, and who knew what buried treasure, still-undiscovered or, perhaps, discovered but unreported. Illegal, but these things happen.

It would have happened in reverse, if she and Henry had ever discovered anything in their garden. Uncle Wilfred had made no bones about that. 'Dig as much as you like,' he'd said, a flash of humour lighting his lean sardonic face, 'but, remember, if you find anything, we're covering it all up again and forgetting about it. I'll not have hordes of bloody archaeologists swarming in to excavate and ruining my peace and quiet.'

'But there might be something wonderful down there,' Margot had protested. 'There's so much of ancient Verulamium still to be discovered. We could find anything!'

'You can find the Temple of Apollo and the temple of every other god they had, but if they're buried in my land, they're going to stay buried. I want a quiet life – and I intend to have it.'

Alas, poor Wilfred. His quiet life had been shattered irretrievably, in a way that could not be buried or covered up. His lean sardonic face had puffed out, buried in the rolls of fat from comfort eating that could bring no real comfort. His peaceful world had gone for ever –

along with his beloved twin daughters, his former pride and joy.

'Ah, yes, the Centurion . . .' Henry chuckled reminiscently. 'We really had them going with that one.'

'Poor Uncle Wilfred.' Looking back with adult hindsight, Margot realised why Uncle Wilfred had been so upset about it. Uncovered ruins could be covered up again, but a ghost stalking the garden was beyond his control. One whisper of a haunting and both media and ghost-hunters would have been unleashed.

'Mother wasn't very happy about it, either,' Henry said.

'So she wasn't. You know, sometimes I have difficulty in remembering that Aunt Christa is your mother.'

'I know.' Henry smiled ruefully. 'So do I. She isn't very maternal, is she?'

'Whatever that is.' Margot had often wondered how she would have fared if Sylvia, her own mother, had lived to raise her. 'I don't think any of the women in our family are very maternal – except for Milly, of course. Milly is maternal enough for all of them.' Or was. There was little sign of Milly's maternal nature at present.

'Ah, well, mustn't grumble, eh?' Henry reached out and clasped her hand, renewing the old alliance.

Dear Henry, the brother she'd never had. And she knew that she was the sister of his heart, never mind Fenella and her twin, Justin – they had each other. The children of Christa's third marriage (there had been no issue from the second), they had appeared too late to be boon companions to their elder half-sibling. Apart from which, their father had wanted his children with him, so their early childhood had been spent abroad – until Christa had ended that marriage and, having been granted custody, had promptly ceded that custody to Milly and got on with her own career.

Tikki shifted position in Margot's lap and looked up at her impatiently – she had stopped stroking him.

'Sorry, Tikki,' she apologised. 'I didn't mean to neg-lect –'

'Oh, no!' Nan swept into the library and took one appalled look at the scene before her.

'No, no, no!' She bore down on Margot and snatched the cat from her lap. 'No! Wilfred mustn't find you here, he has enough to contend with right now!' She opened the french window and lightly tossed the offended cat out into the garden. 'And what are you thinking of, Henry? You know the curtains should be closed before Millicent comes in for her coffee.'

Margot caught a glimpse of baleful yellow eyes glar-ing into the room from outside before the heavy drapes swished across the window, closing out the night and everything in it.

'It's all right in the daytime,' Nan half-apologised to Margot. 'But night was when it happened and Milly can't bear –'

The doorbell chimed, more of an announcement that someone had arrived than a request for entry, for the chime was immediately followed by the scrape of a key in the lock and the babble of laughing voices.

'They're here!' Nan said, with what seemed like dis-proportionate relief. 'I wonder if they got anything to eat during the flight's delay, or whether . . .' Her voice trailed off as she bustled from the room.

'They're here,' Henry echoed. His shoulders slumped with relief from tension, his face looked clearer, brighter. He went after Nan without a backward glance. 'It was just an ordinary flight delay . . .'

Of course it was. His half-brother and sister were safe. What else had they expected?

Then Margot was sharply aware that they might have expected anything – from an accidental but fatal crash, to a bomb on board, to a hijacking and/or hostage situation. This was a family that had been so severely battered by Fate, or circumstances, or whatever you wanted to call it, that they had no faith left, in airline, in goodness or mercy, or perhaps even in God.

And who could blame them?

A sudden wave of exhaustion engulfed her, reminding her that she had bruises and wounds of her own to contend with. She leaned back and closed her eyes, yielding for a moment to the swirling dizziness that threatened to carry her into unconsciousness.

'You're tired.' She hadn't heard Aunt Milly come in, but she smiled at the sound of the gentle familiar voice. 'Why don't you go up to bed now? No one will mind. You've had a long day.'

'Perhaps I will.' She opened her eyes in time to see Milly steal a frightened glance towards the french window.

'You won't miss anything,' Milly assured her, with growing confidence. 'Justin and Fenella are just going to have a snack and then go up to their rooms themselves. You'll feel better in the morning and so will they. It's all that jet lag . . .'

It was a little more than that, but this was not the time to go into it. Margot smiled again and gathered herself to face the struggle to get to her feet, run the gauntlet of whirlwind hugs and kisses from the newly-arrived in the front hall and force herself up the stairs.

If she put a little extra energy into rising, Milly didn't notice. Her aunt, she saw, was glancing again at the french window and still held the book she had been reading clutched like a shield in front of her bosom.

Despite her misgivings, she fell asleep immediately. It was only later that the uneasy dreams began.

Claudia came to sit on the side of her bed, tossing back her long glossy hair and laughing. '*Oh, how funny, how funny! Did you see the way he jumped? He actually thought I was going to run him down –*'

Margot writhed unhappily and half-heard her own

28

protesting whimper, almost waking her, but not quite. One part of her mind recognised the moment being replayed from the past, realising that it was the past. Another part fought to keep a grasp on the present, the reality. Claudia was dead.

Dead . . . but the gurgling laugh still rang in Margot's ears, she could sense the hair brush her face as Claudia leaned closer to whisper something, feel the force of that larger-than-life personality vibrating in the atmosphere.

The Centurion had been a figment of active imaginations, but Claudia had been real – and now it was Claudia who was haunting her dreams. Perhaps everyone's dreams.

And not just Claudia. Chloe was there, too, drifting aimlessly on the fringe of the dreamscape. In Claudia's shadow, as she had always been in real life. The shadow twin, with Claudia's face, Claudia's form, Claudia's voice, but without Claudia's personality . . . without Claudia's husband . . .

Was that why Chloe had done it? Jealousy?

I'm dreaming, the small sentient corner of her mind assured her. *This is all a dream. I wasn't even here when it happened, I wasn't even in this country.*

But it was happening again now. Chloe crept out of the shadows, heading purposefully towards Claudia, whose laughter had taken on a mocking, taunting note. Claudia, who had everything –

Light flashed along the length of the sharp glittering blade as Chloe raised the knife and struck.

Claudia stopped laughing, her eyes widened in shock, she stumbled and fell, pitching forward, falling on to Margot, her hair pressing into Margot's face . . .

'No!' Margot choked, wrenched out of her nightmare, dazed and disoriented. But the hair was still there, still pressing against her cheek like a warm living entity. She reached up to brush it away. It brushed back and began purring.

'Tikki!' She sat up and gave a shaky laugh. 'You frightened me.' The clinging shreds of the dream fell away and her mind cleared. 'How did you get back in? Nan threw you out.'

Tikki pranced back and forth across her thighs, head-butted her fondly in the midriff and purred more loudly than ever, clearly delighted to have someone awake and ready to pat him.

'But Nan had a point,' she said softly. 'Uncle Wilfred has enough to contend with right now. From the way he was carrying on about you tonight, the sight of you might just be the last straw.'

She gathered the cat into her arms and slid out of bed, groping with her feet for her slippers. Tikki rubbed his head against the underside of her chin.

The hallway was dimly illuminated by the shaded nightlight bulb plugged into the skirting-board socket beside the bathroom door. Margot paused to get her bearings. Familiar though this house had once been, the reshuffling needed to accommodate the descent of far-flung family members meant that she no longer had any idea who occupied which room. The fact that Fred and Milly had ceded the master bedroom to Lynette was, alone, enough to destabilise all her memories.

Tikki stiffened abruptly in her arms and stared down the hallway at something she could not see. His ears pricked and seemed to turn in the same direction.

She heard it then. A faint erratic sound, muffled but persistent, strangely harrowing. She felt the hairs rise on the back of her neck, yet noticed that Tikki's fur was not bristling. Perhaps he knew something she didn't know.

As she listened, clutching Tikki as her aunt had clutched her book, as though he were a shield to hide behind, the sound became identifiable: someone was sobbing. Torn with anguish, trying to muffle the choking sobs, someone was crying her heart out. Or, possibly, his. Tears had no gender, heartbreak was universal.

Especially in this house. There was a lot to cry about here. An upper lip that had been suitably stiff and impassive during the day had quivered and given way in the depths of the night, when there was no one around to witness it.

Who was it?

What should she do? She shrank from tiptoeing down the hallway, listening at each door. Suppose someone came along and caught her? And if she did find out who was crying – what then? Burst in and offer a shoulder? Presumably, anyone who had given way to those heart-wrenching sobs had done so at this hour because it seemed safe with no one around to hear them.

But her own heart twisted. It seemed inhuman to listen to such pain and not try to do something to alleviate it. On the other hand, any attempt might seem an intrusion into the other person's privacy. Family or not, everyone had the right to their own space. Perhaps especially family.

Frozen with indecision, Margot tightened her arms around Tikki. He gave a small protesting mew, so soft as to be almost inaudible, as though he, too, recognised the need for secrecy. He twisted around so that he was looking over her shoulder and his whole body tensed.

Margot swung around, but there was no one behind her. Or nothing. Gravity suddenly tugged at her knees, her back, her arms, every ligament in her face and body. The old enemy, more overpowering and debilitating than jet lag, fought for control once more.

There was no question now of hunting down the broken-hearted or even carrying the cat down the stairs to put him out. She had all she could do to remain upright.

She was suddenly afraid that, if she didn't get back to her room and lie down, she would fall down. It would be too humiliating to be found lying in the hallway by the first member of the family to be up and heading for the bathroom in the morning. They had enough to

31

worry about right now without worrying about her, too.

She turned and, leaning against the wall, slowly began making her way back to her room. Tikki stared up at her with sudden concern.

'It's all right, Tikki,' she whispered. 'I'll put you out of the window instead. You can make your own way down, can't you?'

A fresh paroxysm of slightly louder sobs was torn from the anguished throat somewhere in the darkness. Margot halted, guilt-ridden at her inability to help, repelled by her inability to throw off the exhaustion. Perhaps, if she hadn't had jet lag to contend with as well as the other weakness . . .

Still, it seemed as though she ought to be able to do something. She closed her eyes, swaying, her grip on Tikki loosened.

His cold wet nose touched the tip of her chin. She opened her eyes to find him looking at her reassuringly.

Leave it to me, he seemed to say, just before he leaped to the floor and darted off down the hallway. She started after him, but he was too fast for her. He turned a corner and she heard him bound down the three steps to the lower level of the bedroom floor. She almost thought she heard the faint creak of a protesting door hinge.

The dizziness tried to claim her again and she stopped and turned back towards her own room.

As she closed the door behind her, she was aware of silence. The crying had stopped . . .

Chapter Four

Margot awoke in the morning with a deceptive feeling of well-being. After the restless beginning to the night, she had slept deeply and dreamlessly. Her energy, such as it was, was restored. If she guarded it carefully, it might see her through the day. When she glanced at her watch, she saw that the day wasn't going to be such a long one. It was eleven thirty already. Jet lag strikes again!

She wasn't the only one. Christa was seated at the dining-room table. The cup of coffee was obviously not her first, a used plate had been pushed aside and she was working on something in her sketchpad with a charcoal stick and pastels.

'Brunch . . .' She waved a careless hand towards the array of covered chafing dishes on the sideboard as Margot entered. 'Help yourself to plenty, there won't be another meal until dinner. Nan thought this would be easiest, with everyone keeping different hours. The twins aren't down yet.'

'Oh . . .' Margot winced before realising that Christa was referring to her own twins, Justin and Fenella.

'Yes, I see. Good idea.' Margot moved along the line of chafing dishes, lifting silver domes to reveal kedgeree, scrambled eggs, devilled kidneys, sausages, grilled mushrooms and tomatoes, hash-brown potatoes and slices of cold ham and chicken. Coffee bubbled in the glass coffee pot and a toaster waited to receive slices from the brown and white loaves beside it.

Margot filled her plate, decided she was probably not up to slicing the uncut loaves, especially as the bread knife looked rather dull, and took a poppyseed roll instead. She carried it to the table, went back for coffee, then sat down and wondered whether she could eat anything at all. Suddenly, her appetite had deserted her.

Fortunately, Christa was too absorbed to notice. Her charcoal stick raced over the sketchpad, a dab with the red and then the silver pastel chalk highlighted a fold, emphasised a seam, suggested a curve. What had been a vague outline was beginning to take shape, turning into a costume to die for. Obviously, Christa had a contract for a new theatrical production.

'Any more coffee?' It was more of an order than a request. Christa was lost in her own world, not noticing that there wasn't a gofer or assistant within miles.

Oh, well, why not? Margot took Christa's empty cup and refilled it. No milk or sugar, she noticed, Christa operated on straight caffeine.

She was just setting the cup down at Christa's elbow when the handbell pealed out an urgent summons from upstairs, causing her to jump and slosh coffee into the saucer.

Christa swore as the sudden noise tore at her reflexes, constricting her fingers and sending a streak of red chalk off the end of the page in an erratic line.

'They're ruining that child!' Christa snapped. 'Sympathy is all very well, but they're going too far!' Her hand was still shaking, setting her charm bracelet rattling, as she lifted the dripping cup unsteadily to her lips.

There was the sound of footsteps hurrying up the stairs to answer the summons. Not fast enough, obviously, for the bell rang impatiently again.

Christa was right. Sympathy for a bereaved, traumatised child was one thing, but 'spoiled brat' was the phrase that came to mind. Then one thought again of why she was being so spoiled.

'She *has* been through a terrible experience,' Margot said.

'So have we all.' Christa was unforgiving. 'It's still going on and she isn't making it any easier for us.'

'I suppose not.' Margot slumped into her chair and picked at the kedgeree. Unexpectedly, her appetite returned. She had forgotten how good kedgeree could be, made with the proper spices, unlike the bland commercial varieties she had encountered where the hard-boiled egg was often the tastiest component.

'Delicious,' Margot said. 'I see Nan is still working her magic in the kitchen. She was wasted in the nursery all those years.'

'Hmmm?' Christa looked up from her work absently and seemed to have difficulty in recognising her niece.

'Nothing.' What it was to be so absorbed in one's work. Margot felt a small pang of envy. It wasn't so long ago that she, too, had been able to slip into that cocoon and be oblivious to the world. 'Just a pleasantry.'

'Oh . . .' Christa shrugged and went back to her sketch.

'Pleasantries, I remember those,' a voice said behind Margot. 'At least, I think I do. It's been so long since I heard one. There hasn't been much heart for them lately.'

'Kingsley!' It wasn't fair! Someone should have warned her. She hadn't expected to see him here. Not so soon, so unexpectedly.

And yet, when she thought about it, where else should he be? Lynette was his daughter, as well as Claudia's.

'Good to see you again, Margot.' He stooped to brush her cheek with his lips. 'You're looking very well.'

'So are –' The lie froze in her throat. He looked terrible. His face was gaunt and lined, his eyes sunken, deep shadows surrounding them, unbearable pain in their depths, too many silver threads in what had been a thick brown-gold mane. She caught her breath, hoping her face did not reveal her thoughts.

'When did you arrive?' She changed tack abruptly. 'I didn't see you last night.'

'Oh, I'm not staying here.' There was veiled reproof in his tone. 'Bit too awkward, in the circumstances. We're putting up at the Roman Arms, but I'll join the family for the occasional meal and, of course, in court.'

We? Her momentary confusion was dispelled by another voice.

'Hello, Margot. You're looking a bit jet-lagged. It takes a few days to wear off, I know. How wise of you to arrive early.'

She might have known it. If Kingsley were here, could Verity be far behind?

In their teenage years, a crush on Kingsley had been part of growing up. Once he had chosen Claudia, everyone had bowed to reality and moved on. Except for Verity.

'She's got a job as his secretary, my dears!' Claudia had screamed with laughter. *'She lives in hope! She's read too many stories about MPs and their secretaries. She hasn't a chance. Not while I'm around. But if anything ever happens to me, just watch how fast she moves in.'*

'Anyone for a refill before we finish the pot?' Kingsley asked.

'None for me, thanks,' Verity said quickly. 'I've had enough caffeine for one morning . . .' *And so have you*, her tone implied. 'I'll have an orange juice, though.' She joined him at the sideboard and helped herself.

From upstairs, the sound of the handbell pealed out vigorously, urgently. They both looked upwards involuntarily and exchanged a glance.

'You'd better go up.' Christa frowned at another line run off the page. 'She knows you're here.'

'Sit down and finish your coffee first,' Verity said sharply. 'There's no rush. She isn't going anywhere.'

'Yes, well, I'll take it with me.' He gave them all a perfunctory smile and left the room.

Verity's lips tightened, then she shrugged and moved over to sit opposite Margot at the table, regarding her with a cool assessing stare. Margot stared back, not quite so impolitely, she hoped, noting with interest that Verity was several shades blonder than when last sighted. Also, she appeared to have received some professional guidance with her make-up and dress sense; she was altogether sleeker and more stylish than Margot remembered her. She was just as complacent, though. How far had the moving-in process gone?

'Are you here to cover the trial for your rag?' Verity was wasting no time in opening hostilities. 'Or as a member of the family? Or a little bit of both?'

'I'm not a journalist,' Margot said patiently. 'I never have been. I do commercial photographic work, freelance. Advertising, fashion, portraits. I've just finished the illustrations for a cookery book and the job before that was a travel brochure for a local Chamber of Commerce. Nothing to do with news, that's another field entirely.' One she might have liked to try her hand at once, but out of the question now.

'Oh?' Verity shrugged disbelievingly. 'That's not the way I pictured your career going. Still, it's nice to know that you won't be feeding the tabloid frenzy with intimate photographs from inside the family circle. Although I understand they pay quite well for that sort of thing.'

Margot envied Christa's detachment. 'I'm off-duty for the duration,' she answered softly, although what she had done to incur such enmity she could not imagine. 'I haven't even brought my equipment with me.' No need to go into the real reason for that now.

'Oh, yes?' Verity looked at Margot's hands pointedly. 'Now that you mention it, I think this is the first time I've ever seen you without a camera in your hands. Did you have to have it surgically removed?'

'All right, Verity, that's quite enough!' Christa wasn't so oblivious, after all, although the voice could have been her sister Emmeline's. Margot realised that, for all her artistic airs and graces Christa would have had no trouble in controlling a schoolful of unruly students. The icy glare she levelled at Verity could have quelled a riot.

'Sorry,' Verity muttered, as though she had been ordered to apologise and resented it.

Christa kept her cold gaze on Verity for another long moment before dismissing her with a twitch of the eyebrows and returning to her sketch.

'I must see if Kingsley needs me.' Released, Verity pushed back her chair and darted from the room.

'What's the matter with her?' Margot asked herself softly. 'What did I ever do to her? Why does she hate me so?'

'Jealousy.' Surprisingly, Christa answered, although she did not look up from her sketchpad. 'It's not just you. She hates all of us.'

'But why?'

'Because we're Claudia's family. And Claudia had what she could never have and never will have. Jealous little cow!'

Kingsley . . .

'That's why she's here now, not just because Kingsley is here. It's because she's gloating over us. She's glorying in watching us laid low, brought down a peg, the mighty fallen, or however she describes it to herself in her grubby little mind. She's enjoying our pain – and she wouldn't miss it for the world!' Christa tore the page off her pad and tucked it behind the other completed sketches at the back of the pad.

'That's that!' Emmeline swept into the room and slammed a textbook and notebook down on the table. 'There'll be no more work out of her today. She's too excited at seeing her father and, after he's left, she'll be too upset.' Emmeline went over to the sideboard and looked at the empty coffeepot. 'No coffee?'

'Kingsley finished it,' Christa told her.

'Typical! And he couldn't be bothered to refill it . . . or ask Verity to.'

'I don't think Verity would consider that one of her duties.' Christa exchanged a long meaningful look with Emmeline before returning her attention to her pad and beginning a new sketch.

'I'm glad they had the decency not to stay here,' Emmeline sniffed and took the coffee pot off to the kitchen to start a fresh pot.

Margot found, to her surprise, that she had eaten almost all of her kedgeree and was actually looking forward to a second cup of coffee. Perhaps this was truly going to be one of her better days.

'What are your plans for the day?' Emmeline, returning, had her own little ways of letting someone know that they weren't expected to mope around the house all day.

'I thought I might go downtown and stroll around, revisit some of my favourite places, see what changes there've been since I've been gone . . .'

'Wallowing in nostalgia,' Emmeline summed up. 'You might just as well. Once the trial starts, we won't be able to call our lives our own. There'll always be some grubby little journo lurking around, hoping to catch us off-guard.'

That would be some hope, with Emmeline. Generations of schoolgirls had tried their best to do that. Without success, of course. Emmeline had enlivened countless holiday breaks at home with stories of their attempts. From garter snakes slipped into her bed, to the more serious misdemeanours, such as placing an overloaded waste basket outside her room and setting fire to it, every disrupting trick an overexcited juvenile mind could dream up had been played to try to shatter her equanimity. Emmeline had coped with it all in her time and her methods of swift and strict retaliation had ensured that no one tried the same trick twice – or any tricks at all, once she had achieved the post of head-mistress.

What a pity that the media could not be so easily dealt with and brought to heel.

Even more of a pity that this family tragedy was such a high-profile case with such sensational aspects. The murder of the beautiful and popular wife of a prominent Member of Parliament by her own twin sister was guaranteed to have the media slavering. Especially as the rest of the family was also well known, each in their own particular field. Only Chloe had not been any kind of high-flyer, content to remain at home, helping out around the house, filling in when another member of the family needed help with some project, working two or three days a week at a local charity shop. In general, living the traditional, if now rather outdated, life of the unmarried daughter of a well-to-do county family.

Chloe, the quiet one. Chloe, who had seemed to be following in Emmeline's wake as a rock for the rest of the family to cling to when life grew stormy. Chloe, who had suddenly turned from a rock to a raging volcano and erupted, unleashing a torrent of horror, scandal and pain upon the family. Chloe, the dependable one. Chloe . . .

'On the other hand,' Margot said thoughtfully, 'I might go up to London and try to visit Chloe.' If it was going to be one of her good days, why not utilise it to the utmost? Who knew when she might have another.

'Oh, no!' Christa raised her head and regarded Margot with consternation. 'No, you can't. Don't even try.'

'Don't even think it!' Emmeline weighed in. 'In any case, the system doesn't work that way. It's Holloway Prison, you know, not the Holloway Hotel. You can't just walk in and ask to see one of the guests.'

'One of the inmates,' Christa corrected bitterly.

'One of the inmates.' Emmeline sighed deeply. 'One of *our* family . . . one of the inmates.'

'*Cave* . . .' Christa whispered the schoolgirl warning, looking over Emmeline's shoulder to the doorway behind her.

Margot turned. Aunt Milly was standing there, smiling vaguely, clutching her book. 'I thought I heard Kingsley,' she said.

'You did. He's upstairs with Lynette.' Emmeline took her by the arm, drawing her towards a chair. 'Sit down. Have you had anything to eat this morning?'

'Eat . . .? Oh, yes. Yes . . . I'm sure I have.' Her voice firmed and strengthened. 'I'm absolutely sure.'

She was the only one who was. Christa and Emmeline exchanged disbelieving glances. Emmeline poured a cup of coffee and set it down in front of Milly, then lifted the lid of one of the serving dishes and reached for a plate.

'Have another little bite,' she coaxed. 'Just to keep us company.' Margot saw that she had cleverly put the serving of scrambled eggs in the centre of a large plate so that it looked like a smaller portion.

'I don't really want . . .' Milly's voice trailed off, it was clearly too much effort to argue. She ate a couple of mouthfuls, then settled for pushing the rest of it around her plate.

Emmeline nodded in satisfaction, obviously feeling that every extra morsel they could get Milly to eat helped.

'Margot –' She turned her attention to her niece. 'Have you tried the mini-Danish? Apricot, raspberry, apple, or how about a doughnut?'

'I'm fine,' Margot said. 'I couldn't eat any more.'

'Did you sleep well, dear?' Milly seemed to recall her duties as hostess. 'Always so unsettling, the first night or two in a strange bed, I always think. And you so jet-lagged, too.'

'I think I still am.' Margot decided it was the best

explanation for any peculiarities in her behaviour, at least, for next few days. After that . . .

'And I slept very well, thank you. It's not really a strange bed to me, you know. It's my own, my childhood –' She broke off as Milly's eyes filled with tears.

'Of course, you've come home,' Milly quavered. 'You're sleeping in your own bed again, unlike –'

'Have another cup of coffee?'

'Finish your eggs!'

Christa and Emmeline spoke simultaneously. Margot sat aghast at the unexpected effect of her innocent words. She had not realised how careful it was necessary to be. How could she have been so tactless?

'No, no . . . thank you.' Milly got to her feet unsteadily, leaning for a moment on the table before straightening up. 'I must get back to my – I want to see what happens next. I'm so worried about Lady Amabel. I'm sure Sir Jasper intends her no good . . .' She left the room still talking, her words trailing off as she moved away.

'Lady Amabel?' Margot looked after her aunt. 'Sir Jasper?' She turned to her other aunts.

'Those bloody books!' Christa's bracelet jangled, her hands were shaking. 'It's all she does these days: read one damned Regency romance after another!'

'They're not all Regency romances,' Emmeline protested. 'She reads straight historical novels, too. It's her way of escaping the present. Don't begrudge it to her, she needs it.'

'But, if she's like this now . . .' Margot felt a cold chill envelop her. 'How on earth is she going to get through the trial?'

'She'll cope,' Emmeline said. 'We all will. We have no choice.'

Chapter Five

They all jumped when the bell rang again upstairs, an urgent, uncontrolled, almost hysterical summons.

'That sodding bell!' Christa threw down her chalk. 'You'll have to take it away from her! You never should have given it to her, in the first place. She'd have come downstairs soon enough if no one paid any attention to her tantrums.'

'That's easy enough to say now,' Emmeline snapped. 'You weren't here to see her at the beginning . . .' She trailed off, obviously struck by a new thought. 'But why is she ringing for us? Her father and Verity are up there with her. Surely, they can get her anything she wants.'

'I'm sorry.' Kingsley spoke from the doorway behind them, making them all jump again. 'There's nothing we can do. She's too . . . upset.' He looked older, harassed and frustrated at his own inability to handle the situation.

'Please, can you go up, Emmeline? She . . . she's slipped back. She was rude, terribly rude, to Verity. And then she began calling out . . . for Claudia. She wants her mother. She wants her Aunt Chloe. We can't reason with her. We can't calm her. She wants Claudia . . . and Chloe.'

'I'll get her pills.' Emmeline left the room swiftly.

'I'm sorry.' Kingsley spread his hands helplessly. 'I didn't realise – I mean, she knows the situation. She . . . she found them. How can she still want . . . Chloe?' He turned abruptly and went after Emmeline.

'That's it!' Christa said into the silence that followed. 'I'm barricading myself in the study for the rest of the day. And you'd be well advised to start off on your nostalgia trail as soon as possible. When Little Madam goes off on one of her turns, there's no peace around here.'

'I suppose so.' Margot felt oddly disinclined to move and it must have shown in her face.

'Are you all right?' Christa looked at her with sudden piercing concern. 'Did you really not bring a camera with you? Nothing at all? That isn't like you.'

'Oh, I've brought a little one. Nothing serious, hardly better than an old box Brownie.' *Her toy*, Sven had called it. Sven . . .

'I thought –' She pulled herself together. 'I thought I might take a few shots around town for a travel article – Quaint Old St Albans and all that. Nothing to do with the family.'

'That's good.' Reassured, Christa's face cleared. Like the rest of the family, she could not imagine someone without a current project to keep them busy, a goal to be striving for. Except Chloe, of course.

Perhaps it was at that moment that Margot changed her plans for the day. Not that she mentioned it to Christa.

'I might be a bit late getting back,' was all she said. 'Don't let them delay dinner for me. If I'm running late, I'll get a bite in town.' She did not specify which town.

Except for a momentary sighting of Tikki on the way to the bus stop (he lifted his tail in greeting and seemed to nod, then turned away upon some business of his own), the trip to town was uneventful.

At the King's Cross Thameslink station, she let the rush of exiting passengers go ahead of her, waiting at the foot of the long flight of stairs until they were out of the way. Until there was no one to observe her dismay and reluctance as she grasped the handrail and slowly pulled herself up to the top, where another flight of stairs awaited her. She paused at the foot of them, gathering her remaining strength and courage, telling herself that they weren't so bad, really, and that she could see the street level beyond the top of them. She was nearly there. Just one more effort . . .

A sudden rush of passengers from the train which had just arrived from the opposite direction carried her up the last few steps and she moved to one side at the top, allowing everyone to go ahead of her. Most of them, carrying heavy luggage, seemed to be heading for the main line station across the street to continue their journeys, either off on holidays or homeward bound. Briefly, she envied them their happy destinations.

She had to cross the street, too, then wait at the bus stop at the side of the great looming station. When the Number 17 bus arrived, she boarded it, waving the pass included in her ticket at the driver. She was grateful for the pass, it saved her from having to name her destination. Not that the driver would care, or even notice, he would have seen it all before.

'The Number 17 is the scenic route,' Nan had written ironically, in one of the few letters she had written to Margot in the immediate aftermath of the horror. 'First, it passes Pentonville, the men's prison, continuing along its way until it reaches Holloway, the women's prison. Imagine – *two* of Her Majesty's major prisons on one and the same bus route! What does that say about urban planning? The mind boggles.'

Margot sat on the shady side of the bus and watched the Caledonian Road roll past, lined on both sides with little shops, many of them spreading their second-hand wares out across the pavement. People swarmed along the street, browsing, shopping, laughing, talking . . . so much vitality.

She closed her eyes for a moment, surrendering to

the overpowering weariness, feeling the ache in the muscles she had forced into action climbing the stairs. What had given her the idea that this was going to be one of her good days? Or had it started out to be and she had ruined it herself with her own impulsive decision to come to London? She had yet to take the full measure of the beast that was mauling her.

'Not a life-threatening condition,' the doctor had said. But definitely a life-diminishing one.

A change in the quality of light made her open her eyes again to find they were passing under a railway bridge. Beyond it loomed a creamy-white Victorian building which made her catch her breath. Could that be it? One of the great penal institutions of England, sprawling alongside the main thoroughfare as though it were just another block of flats?

No, not quite on the street, she saw, as the bus drew abreast of HMP Pentonville. There was a wall along the pavement, painted black about one-third of the way up and a vast expanse of creamy-white above. Behind the wall was an inner driveway and then the prison buildings. Even the bars on the windows were painted that creamy-white. Did that make them seem less like bars from the inside?

On one side of the prison was, cheek-by-jowl, a block of Victorian tenement flats, one of the early examples of public housing for the worthy poor. Which had come first, the prison or the charity housing? Had it been intended: the carrot and the stick? Enjoy the clean, up-to-date, affordable housing – but make sure you remain worthy and hard-working to deserve it. Stray from the straight and narrow – and you might be housed next door, where you will not find the accommodation so greatly to your liking. The Victorians had their own little ways of ensuring that everyone kept to what was considered their proper station in life.

The bus rolled on and she thought she was prepared for the next prison, but it took her by surprise. A vast red-brick expanse appeared to wall off the end of the street but, as the bus drew closer, she saw that it was on the opposite side of the street. It stretched back endlessly, the length of a long city block, blank and windowless.

Somewhere on the other side was Chloe. Chloe incarcerated. Chloe alone. Chloe, from the sound of it, in deep shock and denial.

The bus turned and went past a circular entrance drive with a bar lowered across it and some sort of administration building on one side. Two or three women were strolling out, appearing quite cheerful, accompanied by several small children. Children? Visiting a prison? But this was a women's prison and the children had probably been taken in to see Mummy, or Auntie, or even Granny. Margot remembered reading somewhere that most females were prisoners because they had been convicted of misdemeanours such as shoplifting or prostitution or not paying their television licence.

She got off at the stop just beyond the prison and walked back, grimly forcing herself to walk all the way along the brick wall to the very end. Thirties architecture, probably. Newer, certainly, than Pentonville, but the lack of outward-facing windows gave it a bleaker aspect. At least, in Pentonville, cream-painted bars or not, the prisoners could look out on to the street and get a glimpse of normal life.

The prisoners . . . Chloe. Margot began to realise that she was in something of a state of shock herself. Seeing Holloway suddenly made the whole horrible nightmare real.

That article she had read had also stated that a good proportion of the women had no place being in prison, but should have been in one of the mental facilities that had been emptied and sold to property developers with the excuse that the patients would do better as Care in the Community outpatients. They wouldn't – and they hadn't. Now HM Prisons were taking the strain that the community had rejected.

The mad, the bad, the pathetic and the downright dangerous. And Chloe was cooped up amongst them.

Margot's steps faltered. Heaviness dragged at her heart as it had dragged at every fibre of her being for the past few months. Chloe . . . it didn't bear thinking about. The entire world had gone mad and nothing would ever be right again.

She had retraced her steps as far as the entrance driveway; now something at the edge of her peripheral vision caught her attention. There was something familiar about the figure walking past the lowered bar and towards her. It couldn't be . . .

'Nan!' It was. 'What are you doing here? Have you seen Chloe? How is she?'

'Margot!' Nan seemed equally disbelieving. 'What are *you* doing here?'

'I asked you first.' The childish rejoinder made them both smile ruefully. 'How is Chloe? What did she say?'

'Nothing. I didn't see her. I just brought her some clothes – they're allowed to wear their own, you know. No prison uniform for women. And I thought she might want her navy blue suit to wear at . . . at the trial.'

'And did she?'

'I hope so. I sent it in and waited. She didn't send it back.' Nan dabbed with a fingertip at the corner of her eyes and blinked hard.

'We thought you'd gone shopping.' Margot hadn't meant to sound accusing, but Nan gave her an old-fashioned look.

'I'll do my shopping now. Here.' She took Margot's arm and walked her down towards the shopping centre on the main road. 'Where nobody knows me. It will be easier. I can get more done without people stopping me to talk . . . or having to watch them avoiding me.'

48

The words brought another sharp insight into what the family had been enduring.

'And why are *you* here?' Nan gave her no time to think about it.

'I'm not sure,' Margot confessed. 'I just felt I wanted to see for myself . . . where Chloe . . .'

'We've all felt like that,' Nan said. 'At one time or another, every one of us has . . .' Nan's mouth twisted wryly, 'made the pilgrimage. But, as we told you, she won't see any of us.'

'I know. I didn't try. I just wanted to see the place.'

'We've got the green light.' They had come to a crossroads, shops and stores stretched out in four directions, people thronged the pavements. They joined the crowd surging across the street and Nan continued straight on.

'We'll start here.' A fruit and vegetable stall spread itself across a street corner. Nan briskly removed a wheeled shopping bag from her shoulder bag and snapped it open. 'We'll get the fruit and veg from the outdoor markets,' she told Margot, 'and pick up the meat at the supermarket. The car's in the supermarket parking garage. You're driving back with me, aren't you.' It was a statement, not a question.

'Yes, oh, yes.' Margot suddenly realised how much she had been dreading the endless flights of stairs she would encounter on the way home. It made her dizzy to think of it. 'I'll be glad to avoid all those stairs.'

'Are you sure you're all right?' Nan picked up sharply on the unguarded comment. 'You haven't looked at all well since you've got here.'

'Jet lag.' How much longer would she be able to go on using that excuse? 'It's really hit me hard this time.'

'I don't know much about jet lag,' Nan admitted. 'With all her travelling, Claudia never suffered from it.'

'Claudia was an enthusiastic traveller.'

'Yes, and I don't know whether it makes it better or

49

worse that she was so happy the night she . . . She'd just returned from what she said was the holiday of her life.' Nan smiled wryly. 'Even though Kingsley wasn't with her. She was cock-a-hoop and on top of the world, already planning her next holiday in that place. It wouldn't have suited me at all, somewhere in the Balkans, with people shooting at each other – although she said that was in another part of the mountains. She raved about those mountains, that unpolluted air . . .' Nan frowned at the traffic streaming along Holloway Road.

'I'm glad that her last holiday was the best but . . .' Nan sighed. 'I don't know. Perhaps it was tempting Fate to be so happy, to have everything, even a perfect holiday . . .'

Perhaps such perfection had been the final straw for Chloe. Was that what Nan was trying to say?

Chapter Six

'We're home,' Nan announced over the rumble of the garage door sliding upwards.

'Oh!' Margot woke from the deep sleep of her exhaustion. Just as well she hadn't taken the train back, she might have been carried on to Bedford or Luton. 'I'm sorry. I haven't been very good company, I'm afraid.'

'That's all right. You obviously needed your sleep.' Nan's searching gaze swept over her. 'Jet lag takes a few days to get over.'

'I'm afraid so.' Margot leaned forward and reached for the carrier bags at her feet as the car rolled to a stop.

'Never mind those,' Nan said. 'I'll take them in. You go up to your room and lie down. I'll bring you a nice cup of tea.'

'No, really, I'm wide awake now.' A nice cup of tea and a long session of sharp probing questions. Margot was on to that one. Nan had done it too often in childhood days. No, thank you, not any more. She opened the door and stepped out, taking the bags with her, heavy though they were.

'Have it your way.' Nan went round to the boot for the rest of the shopping. 'Leave those on the kitchen table and I'll bring in the rest and put it away.'

'All right.' A vaguely guilty feeling lapped at her, she should at least offer to help bring in the rest. Nan was older and it had been a tiring day for her, too, but it was quite obvious that Nan had double her own energy level

– and knew it. Or suspected it. Nan knew them all too well. It was going to be hard to keep anything secret from her. Did the others have that problem, too?

As directed, she left the bags on the kitchen table and wandered away. She wished that she could go to her room and lie down but knew that, if she did, Nan would follow like a heat-seeking missile homing in on her.

'Hello, dear.' Milly looked up from her book as Margot paused in the library doorway. 'Have you had a nice afternoon?' She glanced from Margot to the open page, then back to Margot again and, with a faint sigh of regret, closed her book. 'Come in and tell me all about it.'

Half-hearted though the invitation was, Margot accepted it. She sank thankfully into the armchair opposite Milly and smiled at her fondly.

'It's beautiful weather.' That was as much as she was prepared to say about her day, but it appeared to be the wrong thing.

'Do you think it will hold?' Milly asked anxiously. 'The wind is rising and I'm so afraid it will be a stormy night. At the best of times the wind gusts fearfully down by the old duelling oak.'

'Duelling oak?' Margot echoed blankly. This was the first time she had ever heard of such a thing in the vicinity. 'Where?'

'At the top of the windswept hill.' Milly clasped her hands and wrung them slightly. 'So dangerous! No matter how skilful a shot Lord Lightly might be, a sudden gust of wind could ruin everything. And I don't really trust that Viscount he's chosen as his second. If only Lady Samphira hadn't been so naughty, playing them off against each other.'

'A duel . . .' Margot murmured unbelievingly.

'Yes. You know –' Milly was impatient with her. 'Pistols for two, coffee for one.' She lifted her clasped hands from her book and Margot was able to see two crossed flintlocks blazoned on the cover.

52

'Although,' Milly added thoughtfully, 'I don't see why it should be coffee for one. Surely, his second will also have coffee with him? More dramatic, I suppose, even though not quite accurate.'

'I suppose . . .' Margot echoed faintly. *Oh, Milly, Milly, where are you? Where have you gone? Can we get you back?* But would it even be kind to try? Was it better to leave her there in her own little world until after the trial?

And then?

Margot closed her eyes, this was all too much for her. And she had just arrived. How had the others been able to stand it over the past endless year?

A sudden clamour brought her sitting upright on the edge of her chair, eyes wide open, gasping. It took a moment to identify the sound as Lynette's bell.

There were hurrying footsteps ascending the stairs. Someone was answering it already. Probably Nan.

'That child has slept all afternoon.' Abruptly, Milly was back in the present. 'Now she'll be awake half the night. Really, Emmeline ought to know better than to allow it.'

Emmeline allow it? This was still Aunt Milly's house. Margot felt a pang of dismay. Once Milly would not have relinquished her authority to her sister, nor would Emmeline have dreamt of assuming it. It was another measure of just how far Milly had retreated from the world.

'It's been so nice having this little chat with you, dear.' Aunt Milly's restless hands caressed the book in her lap, then picked it up. 'But I mustn't keep you any longer. I'm sure you have so much to do.' She opened the book. 'And I must see what Lady Samphira is up to. I'm afraid the little minx is planning more mischief and she . . .' Milly's voice trailed off as she became absorbed in the open page before her.

Margot opened her mouth, then shut it again. There was really nothing to be said. Milly was lost in another, kinder, world and who was she to insist that she should

53

remain in one of harsh reality? Perhaps life would be more bearable if they all could find alternative, more acceptable, worlds.

The overwhelming weariness dragged at her as she slowly quietly – not that Milly would notice – left the room. Outside, the stairs loomed like Everest, but there was no other way to reach her bedroom.

One hand on the newel, she hesitated. If she went to her room, would Nan come after her? That threatened cup of tea, precursor to a tête-à-tête she would rather avoid, was an ever-present danger.

Of course, she could always lock her door. The thought heartened her enough to send her up the first half-dozen steps before she paused for breath. Why not? If no one tried to disturb her, no one would ever know.

Another half-dozen steps were accomplished on the strength of that realisation.

Even if Nan did try to intrude . . . nearly at the top now . . . she could always claim that the door must have jammed and that she had been too deeply asleep to hear anything.

Sleep . . . With one final effort, she reached the top of the stairs and turned towards her room, the thought of the waiting bed giving her just enough encouragement to keep her going until she reached it.

The sound of a door closing somewhere down the hallway behind her propelled her the last few feet and into her own room. She closed door and turned the key in the same movement – silently she hoped – then leaned against the door, trying to control her laboured breathing.

There was silence outside, the feared footsteps did not materialise, she was fleeing where no one pursued. This time.

Slowly, she pushed herself away from the door and crossed the room to turn back the counterpane and sink on to the bed with barely enough strength left to kick off her shoes and lie down.

A subtly increasing noise level permeating the whole house brought her back to consciousness some time later. The front door had slammed, she recognised dimly. The distant sound of cars arriving and the rumble of the garage doors opening and closing had also impinged on her restless slumber.

The day was over and the men of the family were returning from the City workplace to the shelter of home.

Margot's eyes opened reluctantly and a sigh that was nearly a moan issued from her throat. The next hurdle to face was another dinner with the family.

'Who's there?' Lynette called out as she passed the half-open door. 'Who is it?' There was a faint note of panic in her voice.

'Only me.' Margot crossed the hall to stand reassuringly in the doorway, hoping her rather strained smile did not betray that she had hoped to pass by unnoticed.

'Oh, Margot.' Lynette seemed disappointed. 'I'd forgotten you were here. I mean,' she recovered quickly, 'just down the hall.'

'In my old room,' Margot said. 'You wouldn't remember. You weren't much more than a toddler then.' Not all that long ago, it seemed, but children grow up quickly.

Except that Lynette appeared to have halted her progress and even to be in the process of reversing it. She pouted babyishly at Margot.

'I can remember, but you were only here weekends. Most of the time you were up in London.' A world of abandonment was in her voice. It wasn't only Margot who had spent most of her life in London, in a stylish flat in division bell territory, well away from her only child. ('*So much better for children to grow up in the country with all that fresh unpolluted air.*' And so much more convenient for Claudia not to have a child underfoot.)

'Well, I'm here now and on my way down to dinner. Coming?' It was worth a try.

'I can't.' Lynette shrank back. 'I'm not well. They bring me a tray.'

'Lucky you.' Margot would have given a lot to be able to retreat to her room and be waited on. In fact, she might manage it for a couple of days while her 'jet lag' could be blamed. The downside was that it would be Nan who brought up her trays – and too many questions. No, the price was too high to pay.

'I'll see you later.' Margot began to back away.

'Come and play cards with me,' Lynette called after her, adding wistfully, 'and tell me about New York.'

Kingsley was standing at the foot of the stairs, looking up at her, waiting. Margot forced her hand away from the newel post. She could walk down the stairs without clinging to the banister. Of course she could. Willing her knees not to buckle, her hand not to snatch for the reassurance of the banister, she descended slowly.

'Margot –' He advanced to meet her. 'I'm glad I caught you. If we could just have a word . . .'

'Later,' Margot temporised. 'After dinner. They're waiting for us.'

'Not for me. I have to get back to London. We won't be long.' He took her arm and led her towards the garden. 'We'll have more privacy out here.'

He couldn't mean it! Margot stopped, unwilling to go farther, to go into the garden. The garden – where it had happened.

'Come along.' There was a trace of impatience in his voice. The years had brought him power, the right to command others. He was accustomed to having his own way. 'What's the matter?'

'I . . . haven't been out there yet. Isn't that where . . .?'

'Oh. Oh, I see.' His face changed, as though he had

56

been recalled abruptly from some other plane of existence. 'I hadn't thought about that. Yes. Yes, I suppose it is.'

'You suppose?'

'All right, all right, I know.' The impatience was back. 'Don't pick me up on every word. Anyway, it wasn't right here, it was farther into the garden, down by the pond.'

'I'm sorry, I just –' But he wasn't listening. He had turned and was opening the french window.

'Are you coming?' He looked back over his shoulder.

'Yes . . .' She moved forward reluctantly, but stopped again at the threshold.

'Margot –' He turned and came back to her. 'Believe me, I understand.' His voice clogged with emotion. 'It's worse for me than it is for you. She was my wife, my best friend, my partner, my life's companion – my everything. After . . . it happened . . . I had to force myself to walk into the garden again. It had to be done. A garden, a house, can't be condemned for something that happened in it. If you look at it intellectually, over the centuries there can't be a square inch of land anywhere that hasn't had blood spilled on it. Especially here in St Albans where there were so many bitter battles fought between the invading Romans and the ancient Britons.'

Intellectually. Suddenly, she hated that word. And all the other words he was droning on . . . blood . . . centuries . . . blood . . .

But it had been Claudia's blood. And only last year, not centuries ago. He might be able to distance himself from it this way, she could not.

Yet somehow Kingsley had coaxed her across the threshold and into the garden and the clear night air. She inhaled deeply, conscious of a sense of irony about the situation. Once, she would have been so thrilled to have Kingsley lead her into the garden for a tête-à-tête. Any of them would have been.

But that was in a different world, a long time ago. They had all grown up and moved on since then. Except, perhaps, for Verity. How very annoyed Verity would be if she could see them now.

'That's fine,' he murmured soothingly. 'That's good. You can't turn your back on the world like your Aunt Millicent. One like that in the family is enough.'

'Milly has a right to want to turn her back on the world!' She flared to her aunt's defence. 'And –' No, she couldn't say that. She broke off awkwardly.

'And so do I.' He finished the sentence for her.

'I'm sorry.' Why should she feel so guilty? She hadn't actually said it.

'No, it's a good point. But we all can't just withdraw into another world. It happened, we have no choice but to live with it. It was done and it can't be undone. The best we can do now is try for damage limitation.'

'Damage limitation?' The cold calculating political phrase struck a chill through her. 'Over Claudia?'

'We can't help Claudia any more. We have to think of those who are left.'

'We *are* thinking of them. We've all come back for the trial, haven't we?' She paused, as though listening to an echo. She had said those words before. She realised that she had not thought beyond the trial – not even to the end of it. And the trial was almost upon them.

'That's just it.' He grasped her arm urgently. 'There shouldn't be a trial. It should never have gone this far. You've got to talk to Chloe –'

'Chloe won't talk to anyone.'

'You haven't tried yet! She might talk to you, she always liked you. And you've come so far – that ought to count for something. It might just tip the balance. She must need to talk to someone by now – and you weren't here when it happened. You were out of it all.'

'I had problems of my own.' She hadn't meant to sound so defensive – had he meant to sound so accusing?

58

'That's why you have the best chance of getting through to her.' His hand tightened, she'd have a bruised arm in the morning. 'She might listen to you. Someone has to talk sense to her. She'll trust you.'

'What do you mean by sense?'

'Real sense. Get her to stop the trial!'

'How can she do that?'

'She can plead guilty. That will stop the whole thing in its tracks.'

'But she said she didn't do it.'

'And said nothing else. She couldn't think of anything to explain her position. She was the only one there, the knife still in her hand. The last place anyone had seen her was in the kitchen, using that knife.' His eyes glinted. 'We all know she did it – for whatever reason of her own. Without the trial, there'll be no weak defence, no feeble excuses, no family linen washed in public.'

Just Chloe quietly shut away in prison for the rest of her life, or as good as. What did a life sentence amount to these days? About fifteen years minimum, wasn't it? And Chloe had lost one life already – her twin's.

'I couldn't ask that of her – even if she'd see me.'

'Then you've got to talk to Wilfred.' Kingsley did not seem surprised at her refusal. 'It's up to him now. You'll have to make him see it.'

'See what? What's up to him?'

'It's time to bring in the heavy battalions. I can get him the names of some specialists. He'll have to have Chloe declared unfit to plead. That will stop the trial, too.'

'I can't ask him to do that!' The effrontery of what he expected her to do took her breath away. She twisted out of his grasp. One of Uncle Wilfred's daughters dead – and Kingsley wanted the other declared mad. 'That would be even worse than Chloe standing trial.'

'Would it?' He gave her a hard look, then his face softened. 'You haven't had time to think it through. I've been living with this thing since it happened. I've seen

59

what it's done to Milly – I don't know how much more she can take. And Lynette . . . Lynette. She might have to testify –'

'Surely not!' Margot was shocked. 'Didn't the police take a deposition from her at the time? They'd use that.'

'The police might. But Wilfred has engaged Comfrey QC for the defence. He's the best in the business, agreed, but he has a reputation for caring about nothing but his client. If he decided that putting Lynette on the stand and tying her into knots to discredit her testimony –'

'He wouldn't do that!'

'Wouldn't he?' Again Kingsley's face registered disbelief – perhaps at her naïvety. 'In an ideal world, possibly not. Unfortunately, I no longer believe in an ideal world.'

And with good reason. That world had been destroyed. He and Claudia had been so happy together, so wrapped up in each other, with every right to expect another twenty or thirty years of happiness and achievement.

'I did once,' he admitted. 'I was an idealist. But it's gone, everything has gone . . . without sense . . . without warning . . . gone . . .'

Margot looked away, unable to bear the pain in his eyes. A movement in the shrubbery caught her attention. Someone – or something – was moving stealthily towards them. Then an inquisitive pink nose poked out from beneath a branch to be followed by the lean tawny body.

'Oh, Tikki!' Margot laughed with relief, bent and swept the cat into her arms, a welcome diversion. Tikki snuggled against her and began purring.

'Margot . . . Margot . . .' The call came from somewhere behind them.

Margot swung around to see Nan framed in the french window, waving to her.

'Margot . . . dinner's ready . . . come along.'

'Yes.' Margot started forward, eager to escape. 'I'm coming.'

'You – not him.' Kingsley stopped her, reaching for the cat. Tikki mewled a protest, digging his claws into her sweater.

'Believe me, you don't want to take him in there. It will start Milly and Wilfred arguing again.' Carefully, Kingsley disentangled the claws from the soft wool.

'Oh. I hadn't thought of that.'

'They don't talk to each other much any more,' he said grimly, 'but the cat is the one thing guaranteed to set them off. Everybody's had enough of it.'

Tikki twisted and protested more loudly as Kingsley carried him away.

'Sorry, old boy,' Kingsley said, as he dropped Tikki gently beside a clump of winter jasmine, 'but it's for the greater good. If it comes to a choice between you or us, I'm afraid it's going to have to be you.'

She was conscious of Nan's approving nod as Kingsley rejoined her and they walked back to the house together.

Chapter Seven

She awoke more exhausted than she had been when she fell asleep. A deep lingering depression told her that there had been bad dreams but, fortunately, she did not remember any of them. She had enough to cope with in the real world. She lay quietly, eyes closed, trying to come to terms with her disrupted life.

She was back in England, in the place that had been home to her since her parents had died in a car crash when she was six. In recent years, home was a small New York apartment – or had been. What was she going to do about that? Could she ever return to it? Or were there too many memories lying in wait back there? All the formerly happy memories that had so abruptly turned into dead dreams. Better, perhaps, to close the door on it all and start a new life here. If only she weren't so tired.

Was it possible to start over again and build a new life without the person who had been the centre of the old one? She felt as though she had exhausted the last shred of her frail energy in getting this far.

In the distance, a bell rang urgently. She opened her eyes, realising that this was not the first time she had heard it this morning. It had resounded through her uneasy dreams with increasing frequency. Perhaps it had even been what woke her.

She was not the only one whose life had been completely disrupted. And Claudia had lost her life . . .

The thought brought her to her feet, completely back

in the present. It was Saturday morning and already clear that there was going to be no peace in the house.

'I'll be up in a minute,' she heard Nan call out wearily.

The bell continued ringing in a petulant, demanding way. Clenching her teeth, Margot hurried towards the sound.

'I'll get it,' she called as she passed the top of the stairs.

'Would you? Thanks.' Nan looked up at her gratefully from the bottom. 'I know it's a difficult time for her, but she's running me off my feet.'

Lynette had just raised the bell to ring again when Margot appeared in the doorway.

'I've-dropped-my-book-on-the-floor-and-I-can't-reach-it-come-and-talk-to-me,' she said, all in one breath.

'Not right now.' Margot bent and retrieved the book, although it did not seem beyond Lynette's reach. 'I've got to get dressed and go into town. Why don't you get dressed and come with me? It's market day.'

'No, I can't.' A momentary wistfulness flitted across Lynette's face before it was replaced by an implacable stubbornness. 'I'm not well enough.'

'You might feel better if you came out for a little walk and got a breath of fresh air.' She knew it was a hopeless suggestion, but that momentary wistfulness had betrayed that it was worth a try.

'I'm not well enough.' Lynette slid down under the coverlet. 'Stay and talk to me.'

'Later,' Margot promised. 'Is there anything I can bring you from the market? Is there anything else you want?'

Lynette turned away and pulled the covers over her head. A faint muffled cry came from beneath them:

'I want my mother!'

*   *   *

63

'Best thing you can do,' Nan approved. Margot had the impression that she would have approved of anything that would get any of them out of the house. 'Do some shopping, visit your old haunts, get everything done now. There'll be no chance to move around freely once the trial starts on Monday and the media circus descends.'

She skipped breakfast. 'I'll have lunch in town,' thereby earning more approval.

The house was deserted as she slipped out quietly, although she knew that most of the family were around somewhere. Aunt Milly, she knew, hardly left the house at all. Briefly, she considered walking into town, but she had already learned not to expend her intermittent energy on non-essentials and so waited at the bus stop.

Tikki strolled past on the other side of the street and she called out to him softly. He spared a glance in her direction and then walked on, still huffy from last night's rejection.

'It wasn't my fault,' she said, but he was gone and the bus was there, the door hissing open for her.

The scene was so familiar, so . . . welcoming . . . that she caught her breath as she stepped off the bus, instantly transported back to the laughter and warmth of the past, of her childhood, her teenage years, her youth.

The long High Street stretched out on both sides from the bus stop, bright and colourful with the stalls strung along it, noisy with the shoppers crowding the pavements, browsing and buying, laughing and gossiping.

She was standing by the large barrow fragrant with herbs and spices when she realised that she was no longer alone.

'*The junk stalls!*' Claudia cried gleefully and impatiently in her ears. '*Let's go straight for the junk stalls. You never know what treasure you might find there. Some day there might be something wonderful!'* That was Claudia's creed.

'Nan wants us to get cinnamon, celery salt, allspice and peppercorns.' Chloe had always been the sober and responsible one, that was why she had been given the shopping list. *'We should get them first, while we're here. Then we can do as we please.'*

'Oh, piffle! Look at that queue – we'll be standing here all day. We might miss something exciting! Tell you what –' Claudia's eyes sparkled with mischief – and challenge. *'Why don't we each palm a different item from Nan's list and slip away? They'd never be able to catch all of us – if they even noticed what we'd done.'*

'That's shoplifting!' Chloe's scandalised gasp and look of horror sent Claudia into fits of laughter.

'These aren't shops,' she crowed. *'They're only stalls, probably half the stuff on them has fallen off the back of a lorry, anyway.'*

'That's a terrible thing to say!' Predictably, Chloe was indignant on behalf of the stall-holders. *'You shouldn't –'*

She might have known the ghosts would be with her. Claudia and Chloe had been so much a part of her life, how could she have thought she might escape them? They were – they had been – so alive and lively.

Margot took a deep breath and tried to recapture her first feelings at the sight of the market, but the brief bouyant sparkle had gone out of the day. The faint echo of Claudia's laughter took on a mocking note as it faded away. Chloe's consternation at her twin's antics was no longer amusing.

Hindsight. All these years farther on, knowing what had finally happened between them, turned the memories dark and bitter.

Chloe, so solemn and strait-laced; Claudia, delighting in teasing and provoking her sobersides twin. Had she finally teased her just too unmercifully? Taunted her an unforgivable step too far?

Other people were able to retreat into a merciful

65

amnesia, Margot reflected wistfully, why couldn't she? Even Aunt Milly had found a way of escape with her endless Regency romances.

All she had was exhaustion. Gravity – or was it emotional pain? – dragged at her, weakening her knees, threatening to pull her to the ground. Not here. Not now. She forced herself to straighten her back, stiffen her knees and move along the row of enticing stalls.

The overpowering, not-so-enticing – at least, to her – smells from a pet food stall nearly finished her. The stallholder stared at her uneasily, as she swayed and rested a hand on the edge of the barrow for support.

Giving the woman a reassuring smile, Margot picked up a catnip mouse and paid for it. Perhaps it would help her make her peace with the offended Tikki.

A gust of wind carried the odour of frying onions to mingle with that of bonemeal and dried offal. Margot tried to hold her breath as she moved away hurriedly, not pausing until she had reached one of the flower stalls where a profusion of blooms promised her that it was safe to breathe again. That was the trouble with markets – parts of them were picturesque only so long as you couldn't smell them.

There was still so much of the market to explore; she had not yet reached the Market Square itself, where the street divided and the stalls followed both byways down to the old bell tower. If only she weren't feeling so increasingly weak.

Food! Although her throat closed against the thought, she recognised that she needed food. And a place to sit down for a while. She had skipped breakfast, after all. At the back of her mind, another memory had hovered, of another familiar place she wished to revisit. The short walk to get there would help to clear her head and her lungs and she might be able to manage more than a cup of tea when she got there.

She crossed the street determinedly and headed for the medieval tithe barn that had been moved close to the

66

city centre and transformed into a self-service restaurant, popular for lunch and teas.

'*Oh, yes, let's go to Waterend Barn!*' Claudia was back. '*They have the best loos in town.*'

'*The food is good, too.*' Chloe followed in her wake, disapproving, distrusting, suspecting her twin was just going to use the loo and not patronise the restaurant.

What must it have been like for Chloe to be linked for life by an accident of birth to a twin she must inescapably love, but largely disapproved of? Would life have been easier for her if she had inherited the same bubbly personality? Or would that have led to even greater sibling rivalry?

Margot took a tray from the rack and joined the queue moving slowly along the counter. She hadn't thought she'd be able to eat anything but, suddenly, everything looked tempting. In a fit of nursery nostalgia, she chose roast lamb with bubble-and-squeak. Deciding that nostalgia bestowed the right to be gastronomically incorrect, she indicated a Yorkshire pudding to be added to her plate and nodded for gravy to be ladled over all. She exercised restraint by taking a cup of black coffee and carried her tray the length of the long vaulted room to one of the tables by the great fireplace at the end.

She unloaded her tray and placed it on an empty table, as the others were doing, sat down and looked around with satisfaction. It was as she had remembered it. Oh, perhaps the flags and banners had been replaced – the colours looked brighter – but they were still suspended from the dark beams. A comforting sense of history and continuity enfolded her; the babble of familiar accents soothed her. So much had changed, it was good to find something that had remained the same. Including the familiar comfort food. She cut a piece of lamb, piled some bubble-and-squeak on the back of her fork, added a dollop of gravy and closed her eyes to savour the blend of flavours melting in her mouth. She was beginning to feel stronger again. She had needed this opportunity to sit down, the hot comforting meal, the chance to be alone and have some time to herself.

'Margot, I thought I'd find you here.'

The voice was crisp, self-assured and self-congratulatory. Margot heard a tray being set down opposite her, a chair being pulled out, the soft thump and gasp of satisfaction as someone invaded her privacy. No friendly ghosts here, but a solid corporeal presence determined to make itself felt.

'Verity.' She did not need to open her eyes to know that she was right. She opened them to arrange another mouthful on her fork, but the flavour had gone from her meal, she was no longer hungry.

'I hope you don't mind my joining you.' Verity didn't care what she minded. Verity was going to do just as Verity pleased.

Margot remained silent, but Verity was unconcerned.

'I'm so glad we have this opportunity to talk,' she said, arranging her glass of white wine and plate of prawn salad in front of her. 'Away from the family, I mean. So that we can be sure we won't be disturbed.'

'Interrupted,' Margot corrected, she was already disturbed.

'Whatever.' Verity gave an indifferent shrug. 'Kingsley told me he'd spoken to you last night. I hope you're going to be reasonable about his request. You know he has the family's best interests at heart.'

'Chloe is part of the family, too,' Margot pointed out. Kingsley seemed to have overlooked that.

'I'd say Chloe has resigned from the family – if not from the whole human race!' Verity allowed a glimpse of her claws. 'Fratricide has to be even worse than ordinary murder. I don't see how she could have done it.'

'Neither do we.' *But aren't you glad she did? Otherwise, you'd never have stood a chance with Kingsley.* 'That's why the trial will go ahead. We might find out why –'

'You'll find out nothing! Chloe was always a bit strange – you don't need a trial to tell you that. It will only stir up terrible memories, provide a field day for the media – and throw Milly and Lynette over the edge into complete madness!' Verity glared across the table before realising that her voice had risen and several people at surrounding tables had stopped their conversations and were avidly eavesdropping. She raised her gaze to the tapestry scene over the fireplace and took a deep draught of her wine.

She was making a scene – the one thing well-brought-up girls dreaded and had been schooled to avoid. The chilled wine brought a red flush to Verity's cheeks – or could it be embarrassment?

'I'm afraid Kingsley overestimates my influence.' Margot spoke quietly. 'I've been away from the family for years now. I can't walk back in and begin telling Uncle Wilfred what to do. Even if I tried, he'd pay no attention to me. And quite rightly.'

'You don't intend to try.'

'No.' Margot met the accusing gaze. 'I wouldn't be so presumptuous.'

'You think I'm presumptuous?' The ugly flush was spreading.

'Did Kingsley ask you to speak to me about this?' Margot countered with a question of her own, suspecting she already knew the answer. Verity had always been one for taking things on herself.

'What difference does it make? You know he's right. You're just a coward! You're afraid of your precious family. Perhaps you think they'll throw you out if you don't toe the party line!'

'Verity!' Margot sent a warning glance towards their eager audience.

'Don't worry, I'm leaving!' The childish petulance was offset by the oddly adult way she drained her glass before pushing back her chair. 'Just remember, I tried.'

69

'I'll remember.' Margot wondered if it was the first drink Verity had had today.

'And remember you'll be sorry.' Verity moved off unsteadily, the final words drifting back over her shoulder. 'Very sorry.'

Margot watched her picking her way carefully through the chairs and tables and wondered. Perhaps life with Kingsley wasn't the rapturous experience they had imagined it would be in their moonstruck youth.

Or was it just that Claudia was a hard act to follow?

Chapter Eight

The encounter with Verity had left her even more exhausted and she lost the little appetite she had had. Ignoring the curious glances from those around her, she picked at her food just long enough to give Verity time to get clear of the building, then left it herself.

Still fighting the debilitating tiredness, she explored a few more stalls and shops, making some desultory purchases, before giving up and hailing a taxi.

The house still seemed deserted when the taxi dropped her at the end of the drive, so that she could make an inconspicuous return. She cut through the little rose arbour to take the path to the back door.

There was a delicious smell wafting through the kitchen, signalling that Nan had been busy, even though there was no sign of her. Apple crumble, perhaps, it was one of Uncle Wilfred's favourites. In the distance, a telephone began ringing and went unanswered, with not even the click of an answering machine cutting in to take a message. She briefly contemplated answering it herself, but it seemed too much effort. She was going to need all her strength to get up the stairs to her room and lie down.

'The telephone's ringing,' Lynette called out plaintively as she reached the top of the stairs. Had that creak from the third step from the top betrayed her? She hesitated, still hoping to slip past unnoticed.

'Isn't anyone going to answer it?' Lynette called again,

in a tone that suggested that she might begin ringing her own bell again. 'It might be for me.'

'Hello, Lynnie, what's the matter?' Margot paused in the doorway.

'The telephone –' Lynette indicated the instrument on the far side of room, still ringing insistently. 'Get it for me . . . please.'

With a nod, Margot obediently crossed the room, wondering why Lynette did not have her own mobile, which would surely be the best thing for an invalid. Or perhaps, she realised, that would merely point up the fact that Lynette was losing contact with her own generation and had no close school friends to ring up and gossip with.

'I beg your pardon?' The crisp barrage of questions shot at her after she said, 'Hello?' momentarily stunned her.

'I'll take it.' Lynette held out her hand imperiously.

'Just a moment –' Margot disentangled the extra-long cord and carried the telephone over to her.

'Yes?' Lynette spoke cautiously into the mouthpiece and then listened. Her face shuttered and hardened into an expression no child should be able to register.

'No comment,' she said clearly and slammed down the receiver. 'Quick,' she instructed Margot, 'pull out the plug. Over by the window.' She pointed at a socket next to a floor lamp.

Margot snatched the jack out just as the telephone began to ring again. Obviously, there was more than one reason why Lynette did not have her own number. Media harassment would give no quarter because of age.

'Was it fun at the market?' Lynette asked wistfully, pushing the telephone away from her.

'Fascinating.' Margot returned the phone to its place on the other side of the room. 'And I found a few bits I thought you might like.' She held the bag out enticingly.

'Really?' Lynette sat up higher, flecks of excitement brightening her eyes. She took the bag eagerly.

'Oh . . . thank you.' The puzzle book was glanced at and tossed aside. Not a good choice.

'Sorry, I expect you already have lots of puzzle books,' Margot said. 'Perhaps the rest might suit you better.'

'The rest?' Her interest renewed, Lynette delved into the bag again, coming up with the small cosmetics case. She opened it and shook out the lipstick, mascara, eyeshadow and a small mirror into her lap. She picked up each item and inspected it, a little smile curving her lips.

'Ooooh, yes. Thank you, Margot.' Definitely a success. Lynette checked and approved the pale pink lipstick and applied it carefully, using her new mirror. She eyed the mascara thoughtfully and the eyeshadow even more thoughtfully.

Were they too adult for her? But that was the point of the little gift: to lift her mind and thoughts beyond her present situation. A promise that she was going to grow up, become old enough to use them, step out into the world and find her place in it. Whatever happened during the next few weeks, Lynette would eventually grow out of this childish role and into an inevitable maturity.

Wouldn't she?

Lynette gave a slight shudder, as though she had caught the thought. Or perhaps because the shadow of adulthood had suddenly loomed menacingly behind her and was more than she could cope with. She was already in retreat, in her own way. It was probably due to Emmeline's experience in dealing with teenaged girls that she had not retreated into the more dangerous byways of anorexia or bulimia.

'I'm tired,' Lynette announced abruptly. She replaced the make-up in its case and let it all slide to the floor on top of the puzzle book.

'So am I,' Margot said truthfully, deciding to leave

everything on the floor. 'Why don't we take a nap now?'

'I'm too old for naps,' Lynette pouted.

'Well, I'm not.' Margot turned towards the door. 'I'll see you later.'

She was aware of movement behind her as she left. She looked back to see Lynette leaning over the edge of the bed to retrieve one of her presents. Was she reaching for the safety of the childish puzzle book or the dangerous promise of the make-up?

We all have our problems, Lynette, but some of us have more than others. Sorry, but my own are enough for me right now.

It was dark when she awoke. Very dark. Too dark . . . and the house was too quiet. What time was it?

The luminous face of the digital clock on the bedside table was partially obscured. It had been perfectly clear the last time she had looked at it. She switched on the table lamp.

A tray containing film-shrouded sandwiches and a thermos flask sat in front of the clock. A short note from Nan informed her that she had been sleeping so peacefully it seemed a shame to disturb her. If she awoke in time to join the family later, she would be welcome; if not, her midnight snack was here.

Midnight? The clock said 1.35 a.m. No wonder the house was silent. She had slept solidly from late afternoon until this frightening hour. And she was still tired.

Even more disturbing was the realisation that Nan had been able to come into her room, check on her slumber, rearrange her bedside table and leave provisions and a note without her having been aware of it.

In fact, there had been two invasions of her privacy. Once when Nan had looked in and decided not to wake her for dinner and, again, when Nan had brought the tray and left it for her.

The food was welcome, however. Whatever the clock said, her stomach told her it was high time to put something in it. It had been a long time since lunch and she hadn't had much of that.

The thermos held Nan's home-made chicken soup, rich with onions and barley. The six dainty triangles under the clingfilm were equally tempting: thin-sliced crustless bread, half white and half brown, generously filled with chicken. She lifted one of the top triangles cautiously, Nan had been known to get overly creative with splashes of chutney, pesto or tomato purée, but the chicken was pristine, only a grinding of fresh pepper flecking it lightly. Perfect. Nothing too adventurous for a jet-lagged tum whose owner would want to get back to sleep after her light repast. Bless Nan, even if she sometimes was too intrusive for comfort.

Margot finished the soup, but left two well-filled triangles, draping the clingfilm lightly over them, yawned and stretched, ready to go back to bed.

This time she changed into her nightgown and removed her make-up. She turned off the lamp and paused by the window, looking down at the long expanse of garden lit by the nearly-full moon. About to turn away, she tensed suddenly.

Someone was prowling about down there. As she watched, a hunched figure flickered in the shadows: too large to be the cat this time, too indeterminate to tell whether it was a man or a woman, too furtive to be there on legitimate business.

And what business could anyone have in the garden at this hour? Was it part of the media circus moving into place for some secret filming? Or, given the swelling moon, some disturbed mentality drawn to the scene of a crime?

Not the murderer returning. Chloe was safely locked up in Holloway. Unless . . .

Chloe had denied the murder. Denied it and then lapsed into an unbreakable silence. But . . . if Chloe hadn't done it, then who had? Lynette had discovered her standing over Claudia's body with the bloodied knife in her hands . . .

Lynette?

Suddenly Margot knew the reason for the tension that jangled through the house like the sound of the invalid's bell.

Lynnie . . .? Did any of them – or all of them – secretly wonder whether the situation had actually been reversed? That it had been Chloe who had stumbled upon the scene and found Lynette with the knife in her hand standing over her mother's dead body? Little Lynnie . . .

No! Margot shook her head, trying to clear her mind of the images that were forming. But, once having slipped into her mind, the thoughts were not so easily dislodged.

It would explain so much. Chloe's silence, for one thing. She would, instinctively protective, have snatched the knife away from Lynette. Faced with the unthinkable, the unimaginable, she would have gone into deep shock herself.

And then what? Had Chloe made a conscious decision to take the blame herself? Or had Lynette, abruptly snapped back into her senses and denying, even to herself, what she had done, screamed out her horror and revulsion and brought the others running to discover the scene so damning to Chloe?

'No!' Chloe had reportedly said. 'No!' And then had not spoken again.

But what had the others said? To her and about her? Someone, Emmeline, or possibly Nan, would have rushed Lynette into the house, soothed her and probably sedated her.

What a family conference there must have been before the ambulance – and the police – arrived. How quickly had they cobbled together a decision as to what must be done? And then did it.

Had they removed Lynette's fingerprints from the knife and then reimposed Chloe's? Or had they decided that so many people had access to a kitchen knife that blurred prints didn't matter?

And what of Chloe during this time? Numb with grief at the death of her twin, stunned with horror at the thought that Lynette was responsible – and dazed with disbelief at the way the family was so ready to sacrifice her to save Lynette.

Or had Chloe been a willing victim? Knowing what could happen to a sensitive young girl hurled into the juvenile penal system and willing to protect Lynette from the consequences of her action. Feeling that she herself was older and stronger and better able to cope with the nightmare. Or perhaps feeling that she had nothing else to lose now that she had lost her twin.

Why then the deep and utter silence? If such had been the case, surely Chloe would have been willing to see members of the family, enter into discussions with her barrister, work towards some way of evading the worst of a prison sentence without implicating her young niece?

Unfortunately, the first hypothesis was the probable one. Dazed and acquiescent, numbed by her realisation that the family was willing to railroad her in order to save Lynette, there must surely have been a growing bitterness that prevented her from speaking to them – any of them.

This family wasn't just dysfunctional – it was monstrous! Was it necessary to destroy Chloe in order to save Lynette?

No, they were trying to rescue Chloe, too, despite herself. Guilt-ridden and grief-stricken, poor Wilfred was trying to do his best for both his remaining daughter and his granddaughter. The QC he had retained was

going to cost a fortune – how much was Kingsley con-
tributing towards it?

And no wonder Kingsley was so anxious to avoid a
trial at all. The clever and aggressive Comfrey QC might
not just plant seeds of doubt in the jury's mind, but
actively point the way to the real culprit. Or, at least,
start people wondering: if Chloe were truly innocent,
then who had killed Claudia?

Or had she watched too many courtroom TV dramas?

It was understandable that, having lost his beloved
wife, Kingsley would do anything not to also lose his
dear daughter. All emotional considerations aside, it
would be the sort of scandal that could ruin his political
career. A cruelly murdered wife had brought a large
sympathy vote, but if the woman had been killed by her
own child, the electorate – and the media – might begin
to wonder what had been going on for that family to
come to such a pass. And, without his wife and daughter, his career was all that Kingsley had left.

But it was unforgivable of him to be so willing to
sacrifice his sister-in-law on the altar of political
expediency.

What *had* been going on? Why should Lynette have
killed her mother? Perhaps Claudia hadn't been the best
mother in the world, more devoted to her husband than
to her daughter, more interested in her own pleasures
and preoccupations than in her child, but Lynette had
never been neglected. Even before she had been sent to
boarding school, she had been happy to spend most of
her time in St Albans under Milly's caring wing rather
than in the bleak modern block in Westminster's division bell territory.

There was movement again in the shadowy garden
below. Margot leaned forward, resting her forehead
against the window pane, trying to see more clearly. She
had to remind herself that the Centurion had never
existed, that he was the mischievous invention of two

78

bored children. On a night like this, it was very easy to believe in him.

Who was down there? She resisted the temptation to go down and find out. She had not the energy to get dressed again and she was not going to go prowling around in nightgown and slippers. Apart from which, there was no guarantee that the intruder would still be there by the time she had gone downstairs and out into the garden.

Could it be Lynette? Everyone had assured her that there was nothing wrong with Lynette's legs. Her invalidism was entirely self-imposed, a neurotic retreat from reality that would have to be dealt with after the trial was safely over. In the meantime, did she secretly slip out of the house in the small hours to take a bit of exercise?

That was one question that could be answered without going outside. Margot walked silently down the hallway and pushed open the door that stood permanently ajar. In the faint glow of the nightlight, she could see the silhouette of a figure in the bed. Of course, a rolled-up blanket placed under the coverlet was one of the oldest tricks in the boarding school lexicon.

Margot advanced into the room, then halted as the dark shape on the bed sighed and turned over, flinging one arm up over its head.

Margot retreated hastily on tiptoes. So much for that idea. Lynette was not out prowling about the garden in the darkness. The thought now seemed highly unlikely. If Lynette would not leave her room, why on earth would she want to go there, of all places? She would want to avoid the garden: where her mother had died, at her hand or not.

And that wild idea now seemed unlikely, too. Just one of the waking nightmares that come in the small hours, to be dispelled by the light of day, or the reawakening of common sense.

Weariness dragged at Margot as she regained her own

room and slumped on her bed with barely enough energy to kick off her slippers. Whatever was going on, it was beyond her. She could not think about it, she could not face it. She could not face anything except sleep – and even then she was afraid that she might dream.

Chapter Nine

She had forgotten to close the curtains, so the growing brightness of the morning wakened her gently. There were sounds of life stirring through the house, unlike yesterday. This morning, it seemed, everyone was at home and ready to start the day. She might as well join them.

She sat up and groped with her feet for her slippers. Her toes encountered something cold and faintly slimy and recoiled. She looked down to find the clingfilm that had covered her sandwiches was now draped across her slippers. She pulled it aside and slid her feet into the slippers, looking around.

The four triangles of crustless bread, in varying stages of destruction, were scattered across the carpet. Not a shred of chicken was to be seen and the triangles that had fallen butter side up had been thoroughly licked. It appeared that Tikki had enjoyed a very successful foray sometime in the early hours of the morning.

Margot gathered up the bread and crumbs as best she could and decided that flushing them down the loo would be the most tactful way to dispose of them. To toss them in the waste basket might be to betray that Tikki had been on the prowl or, worse, might make Nan think that her efforts had been unappreciated.

To reveal that Tikki had been in the house again and in her room, despite the fact that he had been uninvited, would be to reignite the smouldering feud Uncle

Wilfred seemed to have with the cat. Kingsley had been right: anything for a quiet life.

Sunday was ordinarily more than quiet enough, deadly dull and boring, actually. This Sunday, however, was different. There was a sense of urgency in the air as she descended the stairs.

'You'll have to hurry,' Nan said, as she bustled about adjusting her hat, 'if you're coming to church.'

'I don't think I am,' Margot said. 'Not today.'

'Suit yourself but, if you don't come today, it may be some time before you do. The siege will start any minute now and we won't be free to move about.'

'I'm too jet-lagged to do any rushing,' Margot said, 'and I was thinking of having breakfast.'

'You know where to find it.' Nan shrugged and turned as Milly appeared. 'Coming to church, Milly?'

'Church?' Milly said the word as though it were in a foreign language. 'Church . . .?' She drifted past, shaking her head in vague bewilderment at such an extraordinary concept.

From upstairs, Lynette's bell pealed out sharply.

'Oh, I can't!' Nan glanced at her watch and hurried towards the door. 'Tell her I've gone.'

Milly continued on her way, giving no indication that she had heard a thing, and disappeared into the morning room. The house suddenly seemed empty again – or as though everyone were lying low.

The handbell rang again, urgently, insistently. It was not going to stop. It was going to disturb the peace of the house until someone answered.

It was obviously up to her – unless she wanted to try to eat her breakfast with that endless clanging as an accompaniment. She turned and went back up the stairs slowly, clinging more tightly to the banister at each ascending step. Pausing to catch her breath at the top, she looked back and felt a cold chill.

Nan was still standing just inside the front door,

watching her shrewdly. Nan had been standing there watching her all along.

Nan gave a cheery wave of encouragement and, this time, left the house, closing the door softly behind her.

'I've been ringing and ringing,' Lynette complained. She was propped up against the pillows, fractious and flushed with the exertion of her bell-ringing. Or was it temper? 'Where's Nan?'

'Gone to church,' Margot said coolly, regarding her in the new light of the suspicions that had surfaced during the night and could not be completely discarded. 'What is it you want?'

'I want Nan! When will she be back?' Lynette pushed the bell aside and looked at Margot uneasily, as though sensing something less than whole-hearted approval.

'I don't know. What is it you want? I can get it.'

'My tray is in the way.' Lynette pouted at the bedside table where the tray occupied most of the space.

'I'll take it down.' Margot picked up the tray and hesitated. 'You know, you could just put it outside the door and then anyone going downstairs could take it down with them.'

'I'm not well!' Lynette recoiled as though she had been struck. 'I can't get up.'

'You get up to go to the loo, don't you?'

'Yes . . . but I don't have to carry anything.' She was being bullied unmercifully, Lynette's body-language conveyed. She sank deeper into the pillows, her eyelids fluttered down, her voice grew weaker. 'I'm not well.'

'You might feel better if you tried to move around more.'

'Are you a doctor?' Lynette's eyes opened and flashed hostility.

'No, I'm just trying to help.' Margot realised she must go no further. Perhaps a seed had been planted. Perhaps. 'Is there anything else you want?'

'Yes. I want Tikki. Where is he?'

83

'I haven't seen him,' Margot replied truthfully.

'He's been here. I can always tell when I wake up. He likes to play with the jigsaw pieces. Yes – that's what else you can do. Pick them up off the floor . . . please.'

Margot set the tray down on a nearby chair and stooped to gather up the scattered pieces. Sudden dizziness overcame her and she sat down heavily on the floor.

'What's the matter?' Lynette cried in sudden panic. 'Are you all right?' She reached for the handbell.

'No, no, it's nothing,' Margot said quickly. 'It's just – I haven't had breakfast yet. My blood sugar is a little low. That's all.'

'You're sure?' Lynette was not convinced. 'You're not . . . sick?' Dying, she meant. Her world had caved in so completely beneath her feet that she no longer trusted the firmest surface, the strongest person. Anything – anyone – could betray her at any moment.

'No, no.' Margot forced herself to her feet and dropped the jigsaw pieces on the table. Cautiously she reclaimed the tray. 'I'm going to get some breakfast now.'

'Is my father downstairs?' Lynette asked abruptly. 'I want to see him. Send him up to me.'

'If he's there,' Margot promised.

'I know he's there,' Lynette insisted. 'I'm sure I heard his voice a little while ago.' She paused. 'But don't let Verity come up. I don't want Verity.'

Who does? Margot stopped herself from actually saying it, but the thought seemed to hang in the air and Lynette was not stupid.

'You don't like her, either.' Lynette exuded satisfaction; she had discovered an ally. 'I think she's terrible. I don't want her to be my new –' She stopped abruptly, not able to bring herself to say the word.

Had Kingsley suggested such an idea to her? Or had it been Verity, trying to lay the groundwork as she pushed herself forward for the coveted position? Would Kingsley actually marry her? Or, after a suitable interval for grief – and allowing the publicity to die down – would Kingsley look for a bride with better social and financial connections?

No prizes for guessing the answer to that one. Her own cynicism startled her. Once, she would never have dreamed of criticising Kingsley, not even mentally. It was, perhaps, a measure of how far she had travelled, how much she had changed.

'If your father is downstairs, I'll tell him you want him.' Aware of Lynette's anxious eyes, she balanced the tray carefully as she carried it from the room. She was pretty anxious herself. At the top of the stairs, she hesitated, wondering whether it would be wiser not to attempt the stairs with it. One or both of them might go crashing down if she tried.

'Leave it there.' Emmeline spoke from the foot of the stairs. 'Nan can collect it when she comes back. You're not used to carrying heavy trays, especially not on stairs.'

'I was a bit nervous about it,' Margot admitted, setting the tray down on the floor and freeing her hand to rest lightly on the banister as she descended. 'Especially as I haven't had breakfast yet and I'm feeling a bit weak.'

'I hadn't realised you weren't up yet,' Emmeline said. 'I'm afraid I've cleared the dining-room. Come into the kitchen and I'll make fresh tea. Or would you prefer coffee?'

'Tea is fine.' Margot followed her into the kitchen, vaguely uneasy, and watched Emmeline bustling about, setting a place for her at the table. What was wrong with this picture?

While the kettle boiled, Emmeline rinsed the dishes piled on the draining board and stacked them in the dishwasher. 'I'll wait until you've finished and put

85

yours in before I switch it on,' she said. Emmeline was not usually so domestic – or domestic at all.

'Where's Nellie?' That was what was wrong. The weekend help, who augmented the au pair, should be here doing all these domestic chores.

'Nellie . . .?' Emmeline closed the dishwasher door and straightened up. 'Nellie doesn't work here any more.'

'But I thought Nellie was part of the fixtures and furnishings! Did she retire?'

'In a way. We haven't seen her since . . . about a year ago. We had to let her go.'

'Let her go? But –'

'Nellie was unable to resist the lure of chequebook journalism. She sold "her story". Only it wasn't hers, it was ours. How we were coping, how Lynette had taken to her bed, almost as catatonic as Chloe. Oh, she told them everything she knew. And what she didn't know, they invented. They printed it in a double-page spread, with Nellie, the "faithful retainer", grinning all over her face at the top of one page. We couldn't allow her to stay on after that.'

'No, I suppose not.'

'We've got by with temporary help from an agency since then but, with the trial about to start, we've cancelled our account. We'll just have to manage on our own until it's over. We can't risk having a spy in the house. It's *sub judice* right now but . . .' Her voice faltered. 'But, once the verdict has been announced, they can say what they like. Especially if Chloe is found . . . if the verdict goes against Chloe.'

Emmeline obviously could not bring herself to utter the word *guilty*, perhaps she couldn't even think it.

'Then they'll write their books about the case,' Emmeline said, adding bitterly, 'They probably have them written already – all but the final chapter.'

They probably had. From the beginning the case had captured the public imagination and the media had leaped gleefully on the delicious irony of a beautiful young political wife and mother being murdered in her family's garden, after having moved unscathed through some of the most dangerous trouble spots of the world.

'*What can you expect?*' Henry had written, enclosing a selection of clippings. '*If it had happened on one of those foreign jaunts, no one would have paid much attention after the first few days. This way, her story will never end. It will become one of those classic crimes they rehash repeatedly and feature in every collection of famous crimes. Still, I suppose this is the way she would have wanted it.*'

Henry was right. Claudia had always thrived on attention – and excitement, her taste sharpened by that first memorable fact-finding tour when the rising young politician and his glamorous wife had been held hostage for forty-eight hours by local insurgents, while the diplomatic community worked tirelessly to free them and a breathless public, whipped up to hysterical frenzy by the media, gulped down every detail.

It had raised Kingsley's profile no end. And Claudia hadn't done badly out of it, either, garnering radio and television appearances and lecture tours about her experience.

After that, their travels had often taken them to the risky regions of the world; at times, it seemed that the Foreign Office's list of no-go areas was being used as their travel itinerary. Even low-risk countries seemed to seethe and boil over if they were visiting, although never again with such spectacular results.

How very ironic that the most dangerous place in the world for Claudia had turned out to be her family's garden; the most deadly adversary, her own twin.

'It will go on and on,' Emmeline prophesied grimly. 'We'll have the repercussions to deal with for the rest of our lives. As though it wasn't bad enough, to have lost Claudia . . .'

They had lost more than Claudia, they had lost a large

part of their own lives. Emmeline had felt unable to continue as headmistress of her exclusive girls' school with an open scandal in her family. Yet she was a strong energetic woman who ordinarily would not have thought of taking retirement until she had reached sixty-five and would probably have gone on into her seventies in a job she loved and could do easily. Now, from a whole schoolful of girls to supervise and shepherd, her life had dwindled down to looking after just one: Lynette. Although it was only too possible that Lynette needed more looking after than that entire school.

'Is that all you're going to eat?'

'Hmmm?' Margot looked up to find Emmeline frowning at the mound of scrambled egg remaining on her plate. It seemed that Emmeline was going to extend her concern to other members of the family, as well.

'You haven't had very much.'

'You gave me too much. It's nearly lunchti –' Abruptly, Margot realised what her aunt was implying. 'Don't worry. I don't have anorexia.'

'Sorry,' Emmeline acknowledged with a wry smile. 'Too many years of dealing with teenaged girls. One always looks for the worst.' *And usually finds it*, her tone suggested.

'Truly –' Margot pushed the plate away. 'I've had enough.'

'We all have,' Emmeline said, taking the plate. She scraped the egg on to a saucer. As Margot watched, she opened the back door and stepped outside; when she stepped back in, the saucer was gone.

'Don't tell Wilfred,' she said. 'He says we shouldn't have anything to do with the cat – it chose to desert us, so let it stay away. The rest of us don't consider it such a personal betrayal, however. We think Tikki should be encouraged to return.' She looked away and her voice wavered. 'It would be so good for Milly, if he did. It might help her to –' She broke off and left the room abruptly.

Margot rinsed her dishes and put them in the dishwasher. She had an unpleasant foreboding that the day was not going to improve. How could it, when the trial started tomorrow morning?

The hours stretched ahead of her interminably. Another good day to get away from the house and everyone in it. Perhaps she could take her camera and get some more pictures of local antiquities and beauty spots.

The thought had just occurred to her when the rain began. The first heavy drops splashing down turned almost immediately into a torrent, veiling the windows with solid sheets of water. Outside, puddles formed around the paving stones and flooded the path. If it kept up like this, the pond would be in danger of overflowing. The rain showed no signs of abating; if anything, the downpour got worse.

So much for getting out of the house. She was trapped. There was no escape.

Escape . . . Chloe could not escape, either. What was she feeling, sitting there in her cell, waiting for tomorrow? She must dread the thought of being put on public display, of having no place to hide from the staring eyes, the flashing cameras. Would she speak at last, or retreat farther into that trancelike state she had taken refuge in?

Exhaustion dragged at Margot – and yet she had hardly been out of bed for two hours. Perhaps she could slip back to her room and have a little nap. How much longer could she plead, the excuse of jet lag? Already Nan was regarding her suspiciously.

But Nan was still at church, Emmeline had disappeared and no one else was around to see her. She had a good chance of making it before anyone else appeared.

Except . . . she had promised Lynette to see whether Kingsley was here and send him up to see her. For that matter, she was slightly curious herself as to whether

Kingsley was going to stand beside his wife's family . . . or distance himself from them. She was beginning to have little doubt about the answer, but surely Kingsley would not keep away from his only child just because she lived in the maternal family home.

If Kingsley were here this morning, it was probably for the last time until the trial was well under way and he had a chance to see which way public sympathy was veering.

With a faint sigh for the lost illusions of youth, Margot turned away from the staircase and went in search.

Chapter Ten

Milly was alone in the morning room, reading, of course. She looked up reluctantly from her book. It was a sub-Georgette Heyer today. It often was, Margot realised. Safe, reliable, happy ending guaranteed and an absence of any genuine pain along the way.

'Was there something you wanted, dear?' Milly broke the silence, clearly anxious to get back to her book.

'I was just looking – wondering – I thought Kingsley might be here. Have you seen him?'

'No, dear.' Milly was indifferent. Kingsley might have been the name of a stranger. She had no interest in him, in what he might be doing, in where he was. She glanced down impatiently at her book. 'Was that all?'

It wasn't, but it would do for now. Margot had no wish to continue a conversation with her aunt – with this shell of her aunt. Wherever the real Milly had hidden herself away, she was no more in the room than Kingsley was.

Milly come back! The cry was silent. Her aunt was gazing at her with polite blankness, as though she were some remote acquaintance who had unexpectedly appeared at the door. There was no indication of shared laughter and memories, no trace of the warm loving woman who had welcomed a suddenly orphaned child into the bosom of her family and helped her to rebuild her life. *Aunt Milly, where are you?*

'If there's nothing else,' her aunt returned to her book, 'please close the door behind you. I'm at quite an exciting bit and I'd rather not be disturbed. Lady Clarice is about to take on Sir Rupert at Faro, he little knowing that she was the cleverest cardsharp ever to be released from Newgate – but he richly deserves his comeuppance . . .' Her voice trailed off as her gaze fell to the open page.

Dismissed, reproved and made to feel like an intruder in what had been her own home, Margot pulled the door shut with a decisive click, then leaned against the wall beside it, her vision blurred by tears.

All centuries but this – if not every country but her own – that's where Aunt Milly was. Far away from the new century that had already treated her so badly and quite possibly had worse in store.

It would not be kind to force her back into the present, with all its attendant horrors – but, oh, how she missed her! Margot dabbed at her eyes with a crumpled paper handkerchief and straightened up.

There were faint sounds coming from the kitchen. Perhaps Nan had returned. Margot turned in that direction; it was time she began trying to pull her weight around here. Helping Nan prepare lunch would be a good start.

But it was Uncle Wilfred standing beside the fridge, gnawing on a chicken leg, half of a cold boiled potato, liberally buttered and sprinkled with pepper, in his other hand.

'Been a long time since breakfast, eh?'

Not for her, but it was sad that Uncle Wilfred should feel defensive about raiding his own refrigerator.

'And it looks like a long time until lunch.' Wilfred gulped down the last shred of chicken and bite of potato, then glanced wistfully at the fridge. Obviously, the other leg and remaining half of the potato were still in there.

'Nan should be back soon, she just went to church. I'd help, but I don't quite know where to start –'

'There's a leg of lamb thawing in the larder.'

Emmeline appeared in the doorway, calm and quite composed again. 'It should be ready to go into the oven now. We can do that. I'm sure Nan has everything else under control.' She advanced purposefully towards the larder.

'Good, good! I'm glad someone has something under control.' Wilfred made a sudden despairing lunge to open the fridge door and wrench the last leg from the chicken carcass. 'Mmmmmf, frmmm, urrrm,' he said, ramming it into his mouth.

Margot stood aghast but Emmeline was made of sterner stuff, or else inured to such bizarre behaviour. How long had it been going on? Quite a while, judging from Wilfred's expanding waistline.

'Sorry.' He swallowed and his voice was clear and distinct again. 'I said: that will take hours to cook.' His sidelong glance at the fridge bordered on the panicked.

'Not a bit of it.' Emmeline was firm and reassuring. 'An hour and a half at the most, if we put it in now, without waiting for Nan.'

'No, no,' Wilfred said urgently. 'Don't wait for Nan. The sooner you get it into the oven, the better.' He glanced at the fridge again, then, with an abstracted air, sauntered into the larder.

'Don't touch the lemon meringue pies,' Emmeline called after him. 'They're for dessert.'

'Never crossed my mind,' he said indignantly, emerging with two bananas. 'I'll be in my study, if anyone wants me. Christa has taken over the library,' he added, with an air of grievance. 'She's got all sorts of odd bods in there with her. Tell her we want to have pre-luncheon drinks in there in an hour.' He wandered off, peeling the first banana.

Emmeline, looking after him, restrained herself to a faint sigh, picked up the two bare chicken bones and dropped them into the waste bin. A dark brooding melancholy seemed to creep into the atmosphere.

'I'll tell Christa.' Margot made her escape thankfully,

hurrying down the hallway towards the library. She was diverted by a nostalgic melody pulsing enticingly behind the closed door of the small ballroom, once so in constant use for parties. How long since it had been used – and who was using it now? She opened the door cautiously.

The twins – the other twins – intent, completely absorbed, moving in perfect unison, glided across the floor, rehearsing the cabaret dance act that had been such a success in London and Tokyo and was heading for Las Vegas next month, come what may.

Oh, shades of Fred and Adele, eat your hearts out. Without a doubt, Justin and Fenella were heading for the very top. A murder in the family would not jeopardise their careers. If anything, the hint of scandal and intrigue might even enhance their reputations. They were just far enough removed from it for it to become merely an interesting sidelight in their professional biographies.

Margot closed the door silently – they were not aware that it had even ever opened – and continued on her way.

The scene in the library was quite different, but no less impressive. The library table in the centre of the room was almost buried under a great swathe of sketches, samples of trimmings and swatches of materials. Three of the most famous individuals in the modern British theatre were solemnly circling the table, fingering the materials, nodding at the sketches, frowning thoughtfully at the trimmings. As one, they halted in their tracks and stared at the doorway.

'My niece, Margot.' Christa introduced her. 'Brilliant photographer. She's been working in the States, had the top magazines fighting over her. They're dying to get her back but, if you make the right offer, she might consent to stay on a while and do the publicity shots for the show.'

They snapped to attention, ingratiating smiles spreading across their faces. Christa gave her a meaningful look before she returned to adjusting the details of a sketch.

She was on her own. And thoroughly bemused by Christa's version of her career thus far.

'Margot!' Sir Reginald Wharton, the producer, advanced with hand outstretched. 'An honour to meet you at last. We've all long admired your splendid work, of course.'

Oh, really? And what did you like best? The breakfast cereal so quiet it won't disturb your thoughts – or your hangover? The eighth-grade graduation in a freak snowstorm? Possibly the kittens and ducklings crossing a major highway, shepherded by mother cat and mother duck, one on each side, protecting their combined brood? Or what about the disposable diaper advert? That was a seminal shot, indeed.

She smiled wanly as her hand was captured and shaken by the producer, the director and the star, each murmuring compliments she was too stunned to return. She looked for guidance to Christabel, who was frowning down at the sketches, as absorbed in her own work as the twins were in theirs. No prizes for guessing whose genes were dominant in their blood. Poor Henry, it must have been daunting to grow up normal in the midst of such egomaniacs.

Except that he hadn't. Christabel had deposited her cuckoos in her sister's nest and flown off to new adventures, new husbands and undoubtedly lovers. By her lights, she had done her best for her progeny by thus assuring them the solid family background they would not have known had she been compelled to drag them in her wake as she worked around the world.

'Good, good,' Sir Reginald said. 'You won't regret it. I realise you won't be able to start immediately but –'

What had she agreed to? Smiling and nodding, immersed in her own thoughts, she must have nodded at the wrong moment. She saw Christa looking at her

95

with the rather surprised approval one bestows on a slightly backward child who has unexpectedly given the right answer. Yes, she had definitely committed herself to something.

The loud clamour of the handbell rang out suddenly, startling them all.

'What's that?' the actor asked.

'The town crier!' Christa answered caustically. 'Someone is going to have to take that bell away from her before we all go stark staring mad! I don't know why Nan ever gave it to her, to begin with.'

Christa's guests, sensitive to atmosphere as they had to be in their profession, exchanged uneasy glances. Sir Reginald looked at his watch.

'Is that the time?' He managed to sound amazed. 'We mustn't keep you any longer.' He smiled to Christa. 'I think we've settled everything, haven't we? More than we expected –' He transferred the smile to Margot. 'As soon as the costumes are ready, I'll let you know and you can get started on the souvenir programme, then publicity as we go into rehearsal. Meanwhile –' back to Christa – 'I hope everything goes well with – I mean, there's a satisfactory reso – I mean –'

'Don't worry,' Christa soothed, 'I know what you mean.' Her smile was rueful as she saw them out.

'Wilfred wants to have drinks in here in an hour.' Margot belatedly delivered her message, relieved that it had not been needed in order to speed the parting guests.

'Right.' Christa's bracelet jangled as she swept the sketches into a tidy pile and turned to the rest of the clutter. 'Help me take this stuff back to the sewing room.'

Margot picked up a length of velvet and cooed with appreciation. 'How soft!' She stroked it gently.

'Oh, it's a no-expense-spared production.' Christa shot her a sharp look. 'Mind you charge them enough for your services. They'll hardly notice a few thousand more quid.'

'Thousand?' Margot choked. 'Few?'

'It's your name. Our name. They're paying for reflected glory.' Christa grimaced. 'Or perhaps notoriety. In either case, they'll cash in on it at the box office, so see that you make them pay for it.'

'I'm not sure . . .'

'That's obvious.' Suddenly she had Christa's full attention and it was unsettling. 'Yes. We should have noticed it earlier. We've all been caught up in our own problems, but you've been having a rough ride yourself, haven't you? For how long?'

'I . . . I'm just tired, that's all.' Margot raised her armload of materials, defensively, hiding behind them. She had not expected the assault on her privacy to come from this quarter. Nan, yes. Emmeline, possibly. But Christa? And yet, behind the casual offhand façade, Christa was one of the aunts, the same blood, the same acuity. She might conceal it better, but Christa was as sharp as any of them. It was no accident that she was such a success in her field.

'The jet lag just seems to have hit me harder this trip.' Margot's voice firmed, daring Christa to disagree with her.

'Oh, yes?' Christa piled ribbons, tassels, buttons, strings of diamanté, samples of lace and bits of costume jewellery into plush-lined boxes and stacked them on top of each other for easier carrying. 'Terrible thing, jet lag. What are you taking for it?'

Margot had never thought she would be so glad to hear the imperious summons of the handbell ring out again, reinforced by Lynette's plaintive cry. 'Margot . . .? Nan . . .? Is anybody there?'

'Come and find out!' But Christa only muttered it. Everyone was only too conscious of what Lynette had discovered the last time she had gone looking for anyone.

'I'll go.' Margot picked up the last swatch and followed Christa up the stairs. 'I was supposed to be looking for Kingsley for her.'

'He's here?' Christa was disbelieving. 'Today?'

'She thought she heard his voice downstairs.' But Lynette must have heard one of the voices of Christa's visitors and thought it was her father's. An easy mistake to make; the timbre of political and theatrical voices was much the same.

'Wishful thinking. You're not going to find Kingsley anywhere near this house until it's all over and the dust has settled. She may have to leave that room if she ever wants to see her father again.'

'Who's there?' They had been keeping their voices low, but not low enough. Lynette's voice rose in panic. 'Who's out there?'

'Oh, for heaven's sake!' Christa charged towards the doorway. 'Who do you think is out here? What's the matter now? What do you want?'

It was only because she was so close behind Christa that Margot saw Lynette recoil. For an instant, blind instinctive terror flashed across the child's face.

'N-n-nothing . . . n-n-no one,' she stuttered. 'Wh-wh –' She took a deep steadying breath. 'Where's Nan?'

'She isn't back from church yet,' Margot said. 'Is there something I can do?'

'You were going to find my father.' Lynette looked at her accusingly. 'Where is he?'

'He isn't here,' Christa said briskly. 'He hasn't been here. He won't be here.'

Lynette flinched, then rallied. 'How do you know?' Her glance was hostile with, yes, still a trace of fear.

Why should anyone be afraid of Christa? Of all the aunts, she was the least formidable. Emmeline was an absolute dragon – but the headmistress of an academy for teenaged girls almost had to be – when crossed. Even Milly could be fearsome at times, especially when she suspected someone of lying to her. But Christa? Christa, with her easy-going theatrical ways? On the other hand, how likely was it that one could rise to the heights in that profession without the occasional show of temperament? Had Lynette had a taste of it before?

'He said he'd be here.' Fearful or not, Lynette was still arguing. 'He promised!'

'He's a politician,' Christa said flatly. 'They'll promise anything.'

Had Christa always disliked Kingsley?

Lynette suddenly squirmed down under the covers. 'I don't feel well,' she announced. 'I'm going to sleep now.' She pulled the covers over her head and turned her back to them.

'Best thing for her,' Christa muttered, leading Margot out of the room. 'Pity she can't sleep through the next few weeks.'

'Does she know the trial starts tomorrow?' Margot asked.

'Of course she does.' Christa threw open the door to the sewing room with unnecessary force. 'There's nothing wrong with her intellect, you know. Only her nerves.'

Chapter Eleven

'You might as well sleep late in the morning, there'll be nothing you can do,' Nan had said as she went to her room last night. *Keep out of the way,* she meant.

'There won't be much happening until after lunch. Wilfred and Richard will go along to the Crown Court first thing, but Chloe will have to be driven down from Holloway and she's unlikely to get there until ten, or later, depending on the traffic. I understand the first thing they do is select the jury. That may take a while, too. The family is so well known locally and Chloe did so much charity work that it may take longer than usual to empanel a jury. A lot of prospective jurors may have to disqualify themselves because they know her.'

Margot had not thought of that complication. Stifling a yawn, she tried to nod sympathetically.

'Go to bed or you'll be fit for nothing in the morning. When we see how things are going, we'll be able to work out a roster, so there'll always be someone there to support Chloe . . . whether she acknowledges us or not.'

'Will Aunt Milly –?'

'The best thing she can do is sleep late, too. Wilfred wants to keep her out of it as much as possible. He . . . we . . . all of us . . . are afraid she wouldn't be able to handle it.'

Nan suddenly looked her age – and then some. How well was she going to handle it herself?

'You'd better get some rest, too,' Margot said impulsively.

'I'm all right.' Nan gave her a wry look. 'What about you? Are you going to be able to sleep?'

'Oh, I'll sleep, all right.' No fear of that. It was staying awake that was the problem.

Well, it was the dreaded morning now. Margot dragged herself up reluctantly from the depths of sleep, knowing, from her very reluctance, that her dreams had been happy. The nightmares began when she awoke.

Even now, fresh ones hovered, spawned by the memory of Christa's ridiculous trumped-up praise for her imaginary achievements in the States. Her career there, her ambitions, had just been ticking over. Until she met Sven and they became a team, their dreams meshing, no future glory too impossible for them. Only Sven had accepted one last overseas assignment – and hadn't come back. Now all she had left of him was hidden in her suitcase, pushed to the back of her closet, the back of her mind, until she could decide what to do with it.

A low dull throbbing pulsed against her left temple, yet there was no pain. Not yet. Cautiously, she opened her eyes. Still no pain, but she became conscious of unusual warmth and a strange furry –

'Tikki!' The amber eyes blinked at her, the tawny paws brushed across her forehead as he stretched.

'Oh, Tikki!' Her spirits rose minimally, the hovering nightmare receded as she ruffled the soft thick fur. His loud answering purr vibrated under her fingers.

'Come on, Tikki –' She slid out of bed and gathered him into her arms. 'Let's go downstairs and see what we can find for breakfast.'

Aunt Milly was walking along the lower hallway, reading as she went, immersed in the total oblivion of her book. Emmeline trailed uneasily in her wake,

101

watching her with an agonised earnestness, occasionally putting out a hand to steer her away from collision with a wall. Margot halted at the top of the stairs, watching their slow progress until Emmeline had shepherded Milly into the dining-room, no more aware of anyone around them than her sister.

Margot waited a few moments until they had had time to settle themselves, then went down, Tikki wriggling eagerly in her arms as the scent of kippers reached his delicate nose. He gave an anticipatory little mewl.

'Good morning, Tikki.' Milly looked up and smiled, the first smile in ages, Margot realised. 'Come and have a kipper.'

'So you've got the little reprobate,' Emmeline said. 'Where did you find him?'

'On my pillow, having a cat nap.' She could hold on to him no longer. He hit the floor and in one bounce was at Milly's chair, pawing at her.

'Who's a little greedy guts?' Milly smiled fondly, putting a kipper into a saucer and deftly boning it. 'Don't be so impatient. It's coming.'

'But the beast is *going* –' Uncle Wilfred charged through the doorway like a maddened bull, caught up Tikki and plunged towards the window with the struggling cat.

She hadn't slept long enough, Margot thought. Uncle Wilfred hadn't left yet.

'Fred – *no*!' Milly knocked her chair over in the rush to rescue Tikki. 'Leave him alone!'

'Sneaking the thing into the house behind my back!' Wilfred fulminated, struggling one-handed with the cat as he tried to swing open the casement window with the other hand.

'It was my fault,' Margot said. 'I mean, I didn't let him in, I don't know how he got in. I found him when I woke up and I brought him downstairs.'

'Fred – stop!' Milly's voice rose in a shriek. 'You'll hurt him!'

'Hurt him? I'll *kill* –'

He broke off and deflated slowly, arms dropping to his side, Tikki dangling limply. There was a momentary horrified silence.

The shutters came down over Milly's face. She had heard nothing, noticed nothing. She turned away to right her chair and pick up her book. They had all ceased to exist.

In one quick squirming movement, Tikki twisted free and dropped to the floor. He dashed over to the saucer Milly had set down for him and, with a defiant glare at Wilfred, began gulping down his kipper.

Wilfred took a step forward, but the fight had gone out of him. 'What's the use?' He looked from Margot to Emmeline and shrugged. 'What's the point of anything?'

'What are you doing here at this hour?' Emmeline watched coldly as he took a slice of toast and buttered it lavishly. 'I thought you'd be –' She broke off, glancing at Milly.

'The QC rang to say there'd be a delay.' Wilfred's mouth twisted wryly. 'It seems there was some sort of big do at the Law Society last night, so they're all making a late start.' He crammed the toast into his mouth viciously.

Of course. To the Law, this was just one more trial in a long procession of such cases. Another day, another job. Outside the court, life went on. For them.

'All right for some,' Emmeline said tartly. The ensuing silence was broken only by the slight clatter of the saucer clicking against the table leg as Tikki vigorously pursued every last crumb of kipper.

There was a faint rustle of paper as Milly turned a page. Wilfred reached for another slice of toast.

Giving up on the empty saucer, Tikki looked around hopefully, avoiding Wilfred's eye. Margot avoided

Tikki's eye, afraid of setting Wilfred off again if she did anything to encourage the cat. Emmeline poured another cup of coffee.

The urgent summons of the bell came as a welcome distraction.

'I'll go!' Both Margot and Emmeline started for the door. They stopped just short of colliding in the doorway and Margot retreated a step to allow Emmeline to precede her.

'She's been awfully quiet, so far,' Margot murmured.

'I think Nan gave her a sleeping pill to keep her out of the way,' Emmeline replied. 'I can't really blame her. I'd have done the same myself, if I'd thought of it. There are times when that child tries one too far.'

Margot could not argue with that. She, too, would have done it herself. Since her arrival, Lynette had been preying on her already-frayed nerves. What must it have been like to have been living with her all these months, dancing attendance every time she chose to ring her bell?

'Where's Nan?' Lynette demanded ungratefully of the two who had rushed to answer her summons.

It was a good question. Margot raised an eyebrow to Emmeline.

'Nan . . . had an errand to do,' Emmeline said. 'She'll be back soon. What do you want?'

'I want to tell her something.'

'You can tell us instead,' Emmeline said.

'No, I can't!' Lynette's lower lip jutted out threateningly. 'I can only tell Nan. And I want to tell her now!'

'Well, you can't. She isn't here.'

Suddenly, Margot knew where Nan was. Standing outside the Crown Court, waiting for a glimpse of Chloe as she arrived with her police escort. *In loco parentis*, as she had so often been in the past, this time taking the place Milly should have occupied. Milly, poor Milly, once so strong and now . . .

'Then where's my father? I'll tell him.'

'Lynette, you know perfectly well where your father is, where Nan is and where most of us are going to be.' Abruptly, Emmeline reverted to headmistress mode, shooting from the hip and brooking no nonsense. 'You know what day this is and what's happening. We all have enough to contend with without your playing up!'

Lynette looked stricken. Tears welled up in her eyes as she stared incredulously at Emmeline. It was quite clear that no one had spoken to her that way in a very long while.

Perhaps it was time they did. Margot found herself siding with Emmeline. Lynette might have had a hard ride but, for her own good, it was time she began toughening up.

'Margot . . .' Lynette looked pleadingly to someone she obviously considered more sympathetic – or a softer touch. 'Margot, stay and play cards with me.'

'Margot has other things to do,' Emmeline said crisply. 'You're going to have to entertain yourself today. You could always,' she added, giving no quarter, 'try getting up and dressed and going for a walk. It would be an enormous help to everyone if you could even bring yourself to come downstairs for meals.'

'No!' Lynette shrank down under the coverlet. 'I can't! I can't! I don't feel well.'

'None of us feel very well,' Emmeline said unforgivingly. 'And we're likely to feel a lot worse before we feel any better.'

Lynette burst into tears and hurled herself to the far side of the bed, turning her back on them.

'I suppose you think I was rather harsh with her,' Emmeline said as they descended the stairs.

'I think she needed it,' Margot answered honestly.

'She's been getting away with too much for too long. I can't blame her for the way they've spoiled her, but it won't do her any favours in the long run. I've had to deal with too many of these little madams who think the world revolves around them. And the consequences when they discover it doesn't.'

The trace of wistfulness in her tone brought home sharply to Margot just how much Emmeline must miss being away from her work, her school, her place in the world.

'You'll be glad to get back to school,' she said.

'Will I?' Emmeline's mouth twisted wryly. 'Get back, I mean. "Indefinite leave" all too often translates into early retirement. Especially when there's a whiff of scandal involved. The last thing the Board of Governors wants is three hundred excitable teenaged girls speculating about the relatives and private life of their headmistress – and whether homicide, like twins, can run in a family. Too, too unsettling for the whole school.'

'Perhaps now. But later . . . after it's all over?'

'Will it ever be over? Do you really believe that?'

No. No, it would never be over. Claudia would still be dead. Chloe would always be the woman who had been accused of murdering her twin sister. The family would always bear the burden of having been the family where two girls had grown up to come to such ends. Everyone had a high price to pay for what had happened.

'But surely . . .' Margot fought against her own growing realisation of the costs involved. 'If . . .'

'If what?' Emmeline challenged her.

'If Chloe is innocent . . .' Or not completely guilty – not of premeditated murder. Realistically, as Wilfred had pointed out, after Milly had left the table last night, the best they could hope for was a verdict of manslaughter. Possibly mitigated by diminished responsibility. In any case, Chloe would not be returning home for a long, long time.

It didn't bear thinking about – and yet, they had no choice. Margot felt such a wave of exhaustion that her knees buckled. She sank down abruptly on the lowest step.

'Are you all right?' Emmeline asked with sudden concern.

Tikki, strolling along the hallway as though he owned the house, now that Wilfred was out of the way, came over to investigate. He rubbed his head against Margot's knee.

'I'm all right.' She kept her head turned away from Emmeline, using the excuse of fussing over Tikki. 'It . . . just all swept over me suddenly. You . . . the rest of you . . . have had more time to get used to it.'

'I don't think you ever get used to it. You just learn to live with it.'

Tikki gave a perfunctory purr then, satisfied with his inspection, gathered himself and darted up the stairs. A moment later, there was a glad cry of greeting from Lynette.

'Well, that will take care of her for a while,' Emmeline said. 'Why don't you go and lie down for a bit? You can join the others in court for an hour or so this afternoon. If you feel up to it.'

'I will.' Margot pulled herself to her feet; she could make the stairs. Of course she could. And she could face a stint in court, too. But – 'Milly . . .?'

'Milly started a new book this morning. It's the first of a trilogy and she has all three. They'll keep her occupied for the next couple of days.' Emmeline's eyes clouded. 'I suppose there are worse things to do than drugging oneself with words. But she'll have to come back into the world sometime . . .'

Aye, there's the rub . . . Margot nodded numbly and turned to face the endless stairs. What would Milly do when she could no longer escape reality? When the verdict came in?

What would any of them do?

Chapter Twelve

It seemed a very small room to harbour such enormous matters of life and death, made smaller by the way it was laid out. The centre was completely taken up by tables and benches occupied by black-robed white-wigged figures talking quietly among themselves. Along the walls, all four sides were sectioned off by pale oak wood partitions behind which were rows of seating on two sides facing each other. At the top end of the room, the partition rose to become the judge's bench, with His Lordship on high, the great Royal Seal of lion and unicorn rampant, carved and painted, hung on the wall above him, firm reminder of the majesty of the law. Below the bench were lesser tables housing the court recorder and the clerk of court. On, one side of them, the witness box with a chair and two microphones waited.

At the opposite end of the room, facing the judge directly, was the only almost empty seating in the room: the dock, where the accused – the defendant – sat alone. A tiny solitary figure Margot could not bring herself to look at.

Chloe. Cousin Chloe, friend of her childhood.

Margot closed her eyes against the swirling dizziness, but could not close out the memories. Chloe: laughing, teaching the younger ones to ride, organising picnics and swimming parties, taking them to the cinema, always there to be relied on to help with homework, provide extra pocket money, sort out misunderstandings. Chloe, who had always been one of the foundation stones of their lives.

Now she was Chloe, the accused. Chloe, the defendant. Chloe . . . the murderess?

'*Court rise.*' A black-garbed woman had entered and given the order. QCs, barristers and all their attendants, the jury, the public, everyone in the courtroom surged to their feet to stand silent as a red-robed figure in white wig entered from a side door adjacent to the bench and walked along the high bench to his seat, dwarfed by the great Seal above his head.

Those directly concerned with the law bowed gravely to him and everyone resumed their seats. One of the QCs stepped forward to the bench and had a quiet word with the judge. They nodded to each other and laughed, actually laughed. What were they doing – reminiscing about the party last night?

Margot clamped down on a surge of irritation. They had a right to their private lives. That was what law and justice was all about: everyone's right to a private life lived in peace. A life that should not be taken from them.

A life for a life. Oh, they didn't hang people any more, but was a life spent in prison really preferable? What would Chloe be like after fifteen or twenty years? What was she like now? Margot braced herself to look, for the first time, at the defendant.

Beside her, Uncle Wilfred twitched suddenly and scrabbled in his jacket pocket, pulling out a roll of peppermints. He stuffed several of them into his mouth before offering the roll to her. She was aware of his relief as she shook her head, there were barely enough for him there. She wondered if he had more rolls squirrelled away.

The momentary distraction had weakened her resolve. It took her another few moments to steel herself again for what she might see. At last, she turned her head slowly and saw –

Claudia!

Margot leaned back and closed her eyes, wondering if she were hallucinating . . . wondering if she had fainted from shock.

They were twins, that was all. Of course they looked like each other. Identical twins. And yet, it had been possible to tell them apart, especially as they had grown older. Little, indefinable things separated them. A bit more flesh rounding Chloe's chin, the quick fluid gestures of Claudia, the faintest difference in the timbre of their voices . . .

Was that why Chloe had refused to speak?

No! It was impossible! Someone would have noticed. Claudia's had been too large a personality to mask. Chloe's slightly diffident air had usually given her away.

No, it made no sense. Why should Claudia want to kill Chloe, any more than Chloe would want to kill Claudia? It would be like killing oneself, an obscure form of suicide. And yet, one of them was dead, the other one on trial for her murder.

'Court rise.' She had to move, to stand, perhaps to bow like the others as the judge left the room, followed by one of the court officials. What was happening now? Was it all over? Had something vital been decided in that brief interchange between judge and QC?

No, no, it couldn't be. The jury would have had something to say, a verdict to give.

She looked at Wilfred, but he was lost in his private world, seizing the opportunity to crunch his mints between his teeth in the brief respite from absolute silence. The barristers, unconcerned, were talking among themselves. Perhaps nothing important was happening, after all.

'Court rise.' The judge was back already. Perhaps it had been nothing more than a sudden call of nature. They were only human. Weren't they?

Wilfred swallowed audibly and crammed several

110

more mints into his mouth. The judge cleared his throat and the proceedings began.

It was all so quiet and civilised. The QC for the Crown Prosecution Service began his address, speaking in so conversational a manner that, standing as he was with his back to the public benches in order to address the jury, he could barely be heard. What phrases drifted over his shoulder to the listening public were so appalling that Margot could only catch her breath. So many terrible suggestions, couched in terms of sweet reasonableness that they seemed almost possible. The very calmness of his presentation defused all the emotion in the situation.

Comfrey QC, for the defence, at the opposite end of the long table, was jotting down notes, bending forward into a sort of box which shielded his notations from any prying eyes. When he came to speak in defence of Chloe, would he, too, be so . . . so bloodless and dispassionate that it relegated his speech to just another form of intellectual debate?

Margot risked another quick glance towards the dock. This time the defendant looked more like Chloe. Unmistakably Chloe, head bowed, eyes downcast, all propensity towards diffidence multiplied a thousand times. Was that what prison had done to her?

Or, no . . . not to her. She wasn't there. Wherever she had retreated to, Chloe was not here. Only the shell of the woman sat in the dock. Was she as remote as she seemed? Was she seeing what was going on before her? The bench, the judge, the jury, the legal teams, the full panoply of the law? Or –?

Beside Margot, Uncle Wilfred suddenly began to shake, then jerk convulsively. She turned, startled and frightened, to look at him. Was he having a heart attack? It would not be surprising if the strain had become too much for him. And surely he had put himself further into the risk category by the amount of weight he had piled on in so short a space of time.

111

His face was turning puce, he clawed convulsively at his throat, his breath came in gasps. He was choking.

He was also becoming increasingly noisy. The judge turned his head to see what was going on. The QC on his feet stopped speaking and listened, testing the atmosphere before turning slowly.

Chloe did not move.

'Down . . . wrong . . . way,' Wilfred choked, lurching to his feet and pushing past Margot.

Realisation dawned. *He'd swallowed one of his bloody peppermints!* Margot got out of his way hastily. He blundered past her, gasping for air, his upper torso heaving.

The court usher rose and, after a quick bow to the judge, came towards them purposefully. Margot turned and fled after Wilfred, aware that Richard had half risen from his seat and was turning his head from side to side, first looking after them and then looking towards the judge, not sure whether he should follow or stay to support his sister.

In one last glance as the door closed behind them, Margot saw both QCs advance to the bench to confer with the judge. It seemed likely that further proceedings might be suspended until they discovered whether they had a medical emergency on their hands.

'*Aaaaaargh . . . aaaaargh . . .*' With the courtroom door closed, Wilfred gave full-throated cry to his distress.

Margot thumped him on the back and continued thumping, although it appeared to be having no effect. She began to be worried; this could be serious.

'Is he all right?' The court usher appeared beside her. 'Does he need medical help? Oxygen? Is it a congenital condition?'

'*Aaaaaargh . . . aaaaargh . . . Yee-ow!*' The last was a yelp of alarm as another heavy blow from Margot sent him reeling across the corridor towards the suddenly insubstantial-looking railing that might not be enough to keep him from plunging over it and down to the atrium floor.

'Hang on!' Straight into Nan's arms. She caught him and whirled him around expertly, clasped her arms around his midriff and pulled him sharply to her.

'*Aaaa – Oooomph!*' A splatter of small circular white objects flew from his mouth.

'Better?' Nan had not released her hold. For good measure, she yanked him to her again, expelling what little air he had just managed to take in – and anything else that might be lurking in his windpipe.

'I think . . . you . . . got it.' His breathing seemed to be returning to normal. 'Thanks . . . Nan.'

'Think nothing of it.' Nan slowly unwound her arms, her face nearly as pink as his.

'Is he all right now?' The court usher was hovering, obviously anxious to report back to the judge.

'Yes, yes, I'm fine.' Wilfred spoke for himself. 'Sorry about that –' He gestured towards the peppermint-littered floor.

The usher dismissed his apology with a wave of her hand. She didn't have to clean it up.

'When did you get here?' Margot asked Nan. 'Why didn't you come in?'

'I'm a witness.' Nan grimaced. 'I have to wait out here until I'm called.'

A witness. Yes, of course. Nan had been there that night. First on the scene. What had been her first reaction: to gently detach the knife from Chloe's grasp? Or to hug Lynette and hurry her away from the terrible sight? Poor Nan, torn between the devastating needs of her nurslings.

'After I've given my evidence,' Nan continued, 'they tell me I can join the rest of you on the public benches.' Nan held Margot with her gaze and asked, 'How is she?'

'I don't know. She doesn't move. She doesn't look up. She just . . . sits there.'

113

Nan nodded as though she had expected no different. Her faint troubled sigh was barely audible.

'Shall we go back in?' Uncle Wilfred was himself again. 'I'm perfectly fit now.'

The door opened just as they reached it and people began filing out of the courtroom. Among them was Richard; he took his father's arm.

'What's happening?' Wilfred demanded.

'They've ended for the day,' Richard said. 'It's four-thirty, after all. We can go home now.'

'Home . . .' Wilfred rummaged for his mints and threw another handful of them into his mouth. 'Home . . .' His voice was faint and wistful . . . and curiously lost. 'Home . . .'

Home wasn't what it used to be; perhaps it never had been. Nevertheless, Margot felt herself relax as the familiar walls closed around her. The inevitable had been postponed. At least, for another day. She wouldn't worry about tomorrow until it arrived.

A warm welcoming aroma of something delicious cooking in the oven floated through the air.

'Oh, good,' Nan said. 'Milly remembered to put the steak-and-mushroom pie in the oven. I hope she's put the baking potatoes in, too. I left them all scrubbed and ready, but she sometimes gets . . . distracted.'

'Wouldn't it have been easier to put everything in the oven and just set the timer on the cooker?'

'Well, it would, yes. But I like to give her little tasks to do. I think it helps to keep her . . . in touch. Nothing that can't be salvaged fairly painlessly if she forgets. But –' Nan sniffed the air expertly and brightened. 'There's something else cooking in there, too. Perhaps she's –'

'Don't get your hopes up.' Emmeline appeared in the kitchen doorway. 'I put the pie and potatoes in the oven and I made the cake. Milly hasn't stirred out of the morning room all day.'

'I might have known it,' Nan sighed. 'I suppose it was expecting too much. Today, of all days.'

Of all days? It was just the first of who knew how many days. They looked at each other grimly.

'You know what happened?' Nan asked.

'Richard rang and told me. They're staying on for another conference with Comfrey and the legal team.'

'They'll be home later,' Nan nodded. 'That's why the steak-and-mushroom pie. Warming it up won't spoil it. I expected something like this.'

'Christa took the – took Justin and Fenella up to London to talk to their agent. They should be back soon.'

Twins had become too emotive a word to be used lightly, Margot noted.

'And Lynette?'

'Fractious. All day.' Emmeline's lips tightened. 'Although she settled down for a bit after lunch and watched some television.'

The sudden demanding peal of the handbell made them all jump. Lynette must have heard them come in.

'She's been quite forbearing,' Emmeline said tartly. 'You've been back for all of three minutes.'

'I'll go.' But Nan looked grey and exhausted. She spoke in a faint martyred voice, her thoughts obviously elsewhere again, undoubtedly with Chloe.

'I'm going up anyway.' Margot was obscurely cheered to see someone looking worse than she felt. 'I'll look in on her.'

'That's right, dear.' Nan gave her a shrewd *You needn't think you're fooling me* look. 'You go and have a nice lie-down before dinner. Tell Lynette I'll be along in a few minutes.'

Shaken, Margot backed away from Nan's sharp eyes and took the stairs at a faster pace than she usually allowed herself. It would not do to show further signs of weakness. Nan might have most of her thoughts occu-

115

pied with Chloe but, obviously, she was still not unobservant of her other 'babies'.

'Who's there?' Why should Lynette's voice always be shrill with alarm when she had so energetically sent out a demand for company?

'Only me.' Margot was surprised to see Lynette pale and shrink back against the pillows. 'What do you want?'

'I thought Nan would come,' Lynette whined. 'She's back, isn't she? I'm sure I heard her voice.'

'She's home, but she's tired. Very tired. Whatever you want, I'll get it for you. Nan deserves a rest.'

'I'm tired, too.' Lynette's eyes filled with tears. 'I want Nan. She promised she'd tell me . . .' Her voice trailed away.

'There's nothing to tell. They selected the jury, the QCs began their opening speeches and then . . . the case . . . was adjourned until tomorrow.'

'Oh.' Lynette closed her eyes. Margot wondered if she should have said all that. Perhaps that was not what Nan had promised to tell her. In that case, the child now had more information than she wanted – and perhaps more than she could deal with.

'Is there anything else?'

'No . . . not now.' Lynette rolled over, presenting her back to the doorway, in what was becoming her usual method of dismissing her lackeys.

Margot shrugged and went to her own room closing the door firmly behind her with a feeling of relief. The bed beckoned and she kicked off her shoes as she crossed the room.

'Ow!' Something sharp and vicious embedded itself in the sole of her foot. She stumbled and limped the rest of the way to the bed where she collapsed heavily and inspected the damaged area.

Bloody cat! Momentarily, she was in agreement with Uncle Wilfred. She plucked one of the ear-rings she had left on the dressing-table out of her not-quite-punctured sole. Tikki must have got in again and been playing with it, abandoning it in the middle of the floor when he got bored and moved on to fresh amusements.

She rubbed her foot, still thinking dark thoughts about marauding cats, then stood and limped across to the dressing-table to replace the ear-ring, hoping its mate was still there and had not been knocked into some secret cranny where it would never be found.

She breathed a sigh of relief to see it wedged up against the mirror. The little diamond-and-sapphire fantasies were the first present Sven had given her. It would have broken her – No, her heart was already broken. In her present fragile state, it might have destroyed her to have lost them.

She wouldn't risk it again. She'd put them away safely until –

The top drawer of the dresser was crookedly ajar. So were all the other drawers. She had not left them in this state.

She pulled the drawer open and looked down at the jumbled mess. She checked the other drawers: things in them had been moved about but they were left in better order. Probably someone had been disturbed when searching the top drawer. But why? What were they searching for?

At any rate, Tikki was exonerated. However clever and curious he might be, he was neither curious enough nor clever enough to open drawers.

Who then? Someone who had been in the house all afternoon. Aunt Milly, supposedly closeted in the morning room with her Regency novels? Lynette, lonely, bored and fractious – but too traumatised to leave her room? Emmeline? Unthinkable – and yet, hadn't she been rather late in appearing? Had enough time elapsed for her to hastily shut a drawer and run down the back stairs to greet them in the kitchen doorway?

Unthinkable, all of it! That way lay madness. And yet

117

. . . the unthinkable had happened once in this house, to these people . . . why not again?

And what about Christa? Or Justin and/or Fenella? Had one of them taken the opportunity to snoop before they left for London?

No! She could not begin suspecting everyone in the house of searching her room. If she suspected them of this, she might suspect them of –

Margot slammed the drawers shut and secreted the pair of ear-rings in the small zipper compartment of her handbag. The compartment that held the key to her suitcase –

Her suitcase! Margot rushed to the closet. Yes, the clothes on their hangers had been pushed aside. The suitcase at the back had been pulled forward. How frustrated someone must have been to find it locked – and how shocked they would have been had they been able to open it and discover what was inside.

The dark debilitating exhaustion struck at her again. She swayed, steadying herself against the door jamb. It was too much to contemplate right now. Nan had been right – she needed to sleep.

Chapter Thirteen

How quickly one fell into a routine, however unlikely the routine. Having pushed her way through the assembled media outside, Margot even managed a smile as she passed her handbag to the attendant at the X-ray scanner and stepped through the metal detector arch into the lobby.

'I won't be able to come into the courtroom with you.' Nan followed her into the glass lift that rose slowly to the next floor under the glass roof of the surprising atrium. The deceptively demure red-brick façade of the St Albans Crown Court building masked a very modern interior.

'I'll have to wait outside until they call me to testify.' She had mentioned that several times already. The calm competent Nan was, in her own way, asking for reassurance.

'You'll be fine.' But would Chloe? That was the question. How damaging might Nan's evidence be? What did she know about that night? Or suspect?

In the lunchroom below them, they could see the legal team snatching a last-minute cup of coffee. Just another working day for them.

The lift glided to a stop at the first floor and they stepped out into the upper lobby. Some of the benches and booths opposite the balcony railing were occupied, but most of the people were standing, milling around, talking in low voices.

Nan perched on the end of one of the padded benches

and looked around apprehensively, chewing the inside of her lower lip. Margot had never seen her in such a state before.

'Shall I go downstairs and get you a cup of coffee?'

Nan shook her head numbly. Margot hovered beside her uncertainly. She didn't want to leave her like this.

'Good morning. Aren't you coming in?' Verity was suddenly with them. 'We can sit together.'

'Hello, Verity.' Margot was able to restrain her enthusiasm for this suggestion.

'Verity –' Nan craned her neck to look beyond Verity. 'Is Kingsley here?'

'Not just yet.' Verity exuded satisfaction at the implied recognition that she and Kingsley were inseparable. 'He has work to finish in London. He'll try to get here for the afternoon session.'

'Afternoon . . .' Nan gave a faint shudder. What would have happened by this afternoon? What sort of evidence were they going to elicit from her before then?

Margot's inward shudder was less observable. The calm, almost cheerful, way Verity spoke about the afternoon had brought home the reality that this trial was going to go on and on. It wasn't something like a dental appointment – unpleasant while it lasted, but it wouldn't last very long.

'Are you all right, Nan?'

'I'm all right.' Nan gave her a wan smile. 'You two go along in, it looks as though it's going to start. I'll be fine.' But her eyes were shadowed.

'I'll stay with her.' Henry appeared unexpectedly. Henry, who had been spending the past few days in London holding the fort at the family business while Uncle Wilfred and Richard worked with the legal team here.

'Henry, dear!' Nan reached out and caught his hand in a grip that made him wince. 'Is everything all right?'

'The business hasn't gone bankrupt yet, despite my

being in charge, if that's what you mean. And Amanda hasn't thrown me out of the flat yet, although I've offered to go. Or, at least, keep out of the way until this is over.'

'She wouldn't do that. She's the right sort of girl.' Nan tightened her grasp for emphasis and he winced again. 'What a pity you two didn't have a nice big church wedding before all of this –' She broke off and turned away, releasing his hand.

'Yes, well . . .' He patted her shoulder awkwardly. None of them were used to comforting Nan, it had always been the other way round. 'It will have to be a quiet registry office affair – and none the worse for that – after this is over.'

Margot caught the predatory gleam in Verity's eye. Henry was not the only one planning a trip to the registry office. What would Kingsley have to say about it?

'They're going in.' Nan looked beyond them and swallowed hard. The court usher had appeared in the doorway and spoken quietly to those nearest. People began filing into the courtroom. The business of the day was about to begin.

'*Court rise.*'

Everyone shuffled to their feet and watched as the judge entered from his side door and walked to his place in the centre of the bench. The court usher bowed deeply, the QCs inclined their heads, conveying deep respect, but not quite a bow – not compared to the court usher. Everyone waited until the judge was seated, then resumed their own seats.

As the usual conference with the bench began, Uncle Wilfred leaned forward to look at Chloe. More discreetly, Margot turned her head as well. Not that it made any difference. Chloe sat motionless, as she had the day before, eyes downcast, head bowed, wearing the same dark dress.

Verity bumped against Margot as she turned to wave

121

at someone in a small boxed section at the far end of their row. Margot looked, but recognised no one.

'Press box,' Verity whispered appreciatively. 'They've brought out the big guns for this one.'

'There aren't many in it.'

'Not enough room. They'll have drawn lots for who actually gets in and then they'll pool their information later. The man in tweed is the best court artist in the business. He'll do some brilliant sketches of Chloe. She's lucky to get him.'

Uncle Wilfred turned a ferocious frown on Verity. Was he reacting to her interpretation of luck, or just disapproving of whispering in court at a time like this?

'. . . call Dorothy Edwina Helston . . .' The business of the court was proceeding.

The court usher bobbed up, bowed to the judge and left the room, returning a moment later, ushering in Nan.

There were a few moments of confusion as Nan, distracted by the unexpected sight of microphones facing her, stumbled into the witness box, then hesitated indecisively over the question of whether she wished to stand or sit to give her evidence. She elected to sit.

A wise decision, Margot thought, given that Nan's knees had been unsteady all morning and a sudden giving way of them, forcing her to sit abruptly in the middle of some question, might have an unfortunate effect on the jury's interpretation of her answer.

Nan's voice was tremulous as she was sworn in, but firmed at the first question.

'I have been employed by the family for –' the calculation seemed to give her a slight shock – 'just over thirty-five years.'

Margot was aware of Uncle Wilfred nodding his head. Yes, that was about right. Richard had been nearly three and the twins six months when Nan had been hired to help Milly. By the time the twins were seven and she might have thought about leaving, Christabel had split up with her first husband and been offered a great opportunity in New York – but not with a two-year-old in tow. And so Henry had moved into the family nursery. A few years later, Sylvia and Roger's car had skidded on an icy turning on a mountain road and a devastated six-year-old Margot had come to stay.

'. . . just what you saw?' The QC looked at Nan expectantly.

Why was it so much easier to think about the past – to think about anything else – than the trial? Margot wrenched her attention back to the present, but she had already lost the beginning of Nan's answer.

'. . . and Lynette standing there. I realised it was Claudia lying on the ground.'

'And Chloe had a knife in her hand?'

'Yes . . .' The answer came reluctantly.

'What was Lynette doing?'

'Standing there . . . frozen . . . they both were. When she saw me, Lynette began to cry.'

'What did you do then?'

'I went to her, of course. She . . . she didn't move. It seemed as though she couldn't. I put my arms around her, told her, "Don't look!", but it was too late. She'd already seen that her mother was dead.'

'And what was Chloe doing?'

'She . . . she was just standing there . . . frozen.'

'Holding the knife?'

'Yes.'

'The bloodstained knife?'

'Yes.' Nan's voice was a whisper, the answer seemed torn from her.

'What did you do then?'

'I took Lynette inside and called the doctor.'

'Leaving Chloe outside? Still holding the knife? Still . . . frozen?'

'Yes.'

'You didn't call the police?'

123

'No. It never occurred to me. The doctor called the police.'

'What happened then? Before the doctor arrived?'

'I told Millicent. I had to. She was their mother. She went out to Claudia . . . and Chloe . . . while I took Lynette upstairs and put her to bed.'

The judge leaned forward and asked an inaudible question.

'A minor, m'lud. We have a deposition.'

Margot was jostled by Wilfred's arm as he dug into a pocket. She glanced sideways to see him pull out a crumpled handkerchief and raise it to his face. Not tears, surely? Rigidly stoic, Wilfred would never give way in public. Probably not even in front of Milly. It must be perspiration –

The working of his jaws betrayed him, as did the faint smell that wafted her way a moment later.

Wilfred was gnawing frantically at a large knob of cheddar cheese concealed in his handkerchief.

At least it was a safer bet against choking than a handful of peppermints.

'Would you like a glass of water?'

Margot looked up, startled, but no one was being sarcastic to Wilfred. The question had been addressed to Nan, who was leaning back in her chair, looking shattered. What had she just said?

The jury were all looking at Chloe, who sat there oblivious. The occupants of the press box were all leaning forward to stare avidly at Chloe. Wilfred's jaws were working so savagely it was a wonder he didn't break a tooth.

Nan shook her head, still fighting for control, then burst into tears.

One of the QCs stepped forward and said something to the judge, who nodded.

'Excused,' he said.

The court usher stepped forward to help Nan from the witness box.

'I'll see her home.' Welcoming the excuse to leave, Margot got to her feet. She had had just about as much as she could stand. The walls were beginning to close in on her, the smell of cheese was nauseating her. She was in serious danger of fainting if she remained in court.

Henry nodded his thanks as he slipped into her relinquished place, the only seat in the crowded courtroom.

Nan caught her arm gratefully as she emerged from the courtroom just behind the usher, who was saying solicitously, 'You're sure you'll be all right?'

What a fragile family she must think them. Wilfred's choking fit yesterday, Nan's disintegration today. And the silent prisoner in the dock – Chloe, the most fragile of all.

'I'm taking her home,' Margot said.

'If . . . if you don't need me any more today, that is.' Nan was apologetic.

'We can always call you again later,' the court usher reassured her. 'If necessary.' She did not mention the possibility, the almost-certainty, of cross-examination.

'I'm sorry.' At the car, still dabbing at tears, Nan held the keys out to Margot. 'I don't think I can manage. Could you drive?'

'Of course,' Margot lied, taking the keys reluctantly. She hadn't driven in months – and then it had been on the other side of the road. 'I may be a bit rusty on keeping to the left, I'm afraid.'

'You'll still do better than me right now.' Nan gave her a watery smile. 'Don't worry. It will come back to you.'

'I hope so.'

Still, she didn't do too badly and felt a mild glow of accomplishment as they swept up the drive and stopped in front of the house.

The handbell began ringing as soon as they were inside the front door.

'I can't!' Nan looked distraught. 'Where are the others? Let one of them see to her.'

'I'll go,' Margot placated. 'You rest for a bit. I'll bring you some lunch.'

'I'm not hungry.' Nan shook her head, then covered her ears as the bell rang again and again. 'Just stop that noise! It's enough to wake the –'

She broke off, aghast at what she had almost said, and burst into tears again.

Chapter 14

Lynette was sulking by the time Margot appeared in the doorway, having first settled Nan in her room.

'I don't want *you*,' she announced pettishly. 'Where's Aunt Emmeline?'

'I don't know.'

'Where's my grandmother?'

'I don't know.'

'Why don't you know?'

'Because we just got in and I haven't had time to search the house, even if I had the inclination – which I haven't!' Margot did not bother to conceal her annoyance.

'Where's Nan?' Lynette shrank back against the pillows, she was not accustomed to impatience. 'I want Nan!'

'Nan isn't feeling well. She's going to take a nap. I'm afraid you're stuck with me. What do you want?'

'I want –' Lynette took a deep breath. 'I want to know what's going on. There's somebody in the garden. They were there last night and now again today. Who's there?'

'Oh?' Margot regarded the bedridden child without favour. 'How do you know someone's there?'

'Tikki told me.' Lynette was on the defensive, she gestured towards the window. 'Look at him. He's seeing someone . . . or something.'

Sure enough, Tikki was crouched on the window sill, looking down into the garden with alert interest. His head turned slowly as though following the progress of someone below.

'Paparazzi!' Margot crossed to the window to glare down at them. Emmeline had said they wormed their way in everywhere.

They were not immediately apparent, however. Even following the line of Tikki's laserlike stare revealed no intruders. Whatever was down there, he was the only one who could see it.

Margot shuddered involuntarily as a cold chill swept over her. *Someone walking over my –* She cut off the thought, feeling something of Nan's revulsion – and for the same reason. All of the old sayings took on a new and grimmer meaning in the light of what had happened.

'What is it?' Lynette cried. 'Who is it?' Did she imagine that her mother's ghost had come back to haunt the garden?

'Nothing's there,' Margot said, adding soothingly, 'Tikki must be watching mice or hedgehogs in the bushes.'

'Ye-e-es . . .' Lynette did not sound convinced, her eyes were fearful. Too fearful. What was she afraid of?

Tikki lost interest in the scene below and rubbed his chin along Margot's hand, asking for affection. She indulged him briefly before turning back to Lynette.

'Is there anything else bothering you?' She thought she had used quite a reasonable tone, but Lynette flinched as though expecting a blow. For an instant, the child looked pinched and apprehensive beyond her years, a disturbing foreshadowing of the neurotic woman she might grow into if she could not find her way through this traumatic time.

And what of yourself? Unbidden, the question loomed at the back of her mind; too urgent to be ignored, too much to face right now. The familiar exhaustion swept over her, the ever-present weakness asserted itself again. She leaned against the window frame for support.

Tikki, quick to sense a change of mood, shifted his position to stare up at her. He looked concerned.

'Margot –' It had even penetrated Lynette's self-absorption. 'Are you all right?'

'Just tired.' Margot forced a smile. 'Very tired. I might just go to my room and lie down for a bit. If you're sure there's nothing more you want.'

'No. No, thank you.' Lynette's voice was stronger at this comforting evidence of weakness in an adult. 'You go and rest,' she added, in an unconscious imitation of Nan. 'That jet lag is a beastly business.'

Tikki escorted Margot back to her room, waited until she had kicked off her shoes and stretched out on top of the covers, then leaped up and settled down beside her.

'I suppose you think you're smart,' she murmured, gathering the warm friendly little form to her. 'Taking advantage just because I'm too tired to get up and throw you out.'

He was still there when she awoke later. How much later? It was dark outside, the house was silent. How long had she slept? Through the afternoon and into the night again? She had intended to rest for half an hour or so and then return to court for the afternoon session. Would she ever grow accustomed to the way in which her own body was betraying her?

She was wide awake now and, ironically, felt a surge of energy. Now – when it was too late to harness it for any particular purpose.

Tikki raised his head and stared at her, then appeared to remember an urgent engagement elsewhere. He stretched, gave her a friendly headbutt and leaped to the floor and out of the door.

The bedside clock said 1.00. Given this darkness, that had to be a.m. and not p.m. She had literally slept the clock around and, she realised, she was hungry. If Nan had looked in to leave a sandwich, she had obviously thought better of it upon seeing Tikki.

Probably she had left something waiting for Margot downstairs. If not, she knew that Margot was perfectly capable of scavenging in the fridge and larder for herself. If Uncle Wilfred had left anything in them.

And the sooner the better. Suddenly ravenous, Margot stepped out into the hallway, dark except for the pale nightlight marking the half-landing. Unusually, Lynette's door was closed, so she must be asleep. Rather a pity that, Margot would not have minded a game of cards or a chat after she ate.

As it was, her excuses about jet lag had caught up with her. 1 a.m. here meant that it was only 8 p.m. back in New York. No wonder she was so wide awake after a long sleep. The only person awake in this crowded household.

Or was she? She paused at the foot of the stairs and listened. Silence, bloody silence. Yes, she was the only one awake. She might as well be alone in the house. Even Tikki had deserted her – as was his wont. There were times when one sympathised with Wilfred's view of his traitorous cat.

All right, so be it. She headed for the kitchen and the siren call of the humming refrigerator. She'd have some sort of snack and then go back to her room and take a sleeping pill to help her finish out the night. It might be as well to set the alarm, too, to make sure she was up in time for the morning session.

She wondered if Kingsley would be there in the morning – or if he had really shown up for the afternoon session. He might genuinely have intended to, but she herself was proof of what could happen to the best of intentions.

'Chicken soup in flask.' Nan had left a note for her. 'Cheese sandwich to be toasted in gadget on counter. PS: Nothing happened this afternoon.'

Comfort food – just what she needed. Trust Nan.

Margot removed the clingfilm protecting the sandwich, lowered the lid and switched on the sandwich toaster. While waiting for it to toast, she unscrewed the cap of the thermos flask and poured out the steaming fragrant soup, chunks of chicken splashing into the cup along with beads of barley and diced carrots. Delicious!

She sipped it appreciatively, retrieved the hot melting cheese sandwich and nibbled it between sips. Just what she needed.

If a little too much. The other half of the sandwich and the second cup of soup seemed a bit excessive. She disposed of the sandwich half and drank the rest of the broth, leaving a good thick residue embedded with chicken chunks which she eyed thoughtfully.

Where was Tikki when you needed him? If he hadn't strayed too far, he was in luck.

She became aware of a chill draught around her ankles and looked across the kitchen to find the back door slightly ajar. Tikki had obviously passed that way.

But Tikki, clever though he was, could not have opened the door by himself. Someone must have closed it carelessly.

Very carelessly, considering that the paparazzi might be prowling outside. Only the silence of the house persuaded her that its defences had not been breached.

Not yet. She crossed to the door and stood listening to the soft night sounds outside. The wind rustled gently through the bushes, the night insects signalled softly to each other.

Was Tikki still nearby? He would enjoy the chicken soup so much. She opened the door wider and stepped outside.

Gradually, her eyes adjusted to the darkness. Clouds scudded across the sky, veiling the moon sporadically. On the ground, shadows flickered silently, deceptively . . .

Was this what Sven had experienced – just before he had driven into the crossfire?

All the horrors she had been keeping at bay swept forward to engulf her, bringing bitterness and desolation in their wake. When she thought of the way Claudia had moved unscathed through uprisings and revolutions, her feelings intensified. Why should it have been Sven who had had the bad luck to be in the wrong place at the wrong time?

And yet Claudia's luck had run out right here in the garden of her childhood home. Home – the place of safety, of refuge – abruptly became an extension of the nightmare world outside. The wind seemed colder, there could be something lurking in the rustling bushes more sinister than the cat.

'Tikki . . .' Margot called faintly, shrinking back against the wall of the house. 'Tikki . . .' A name, a concept, of something warm and comforting that had vanished for ever.

'Tikki . . .' Was that an answering movement in the shrubbery down by the pond?

She pushed herself away from the house, straining her eyes against the darkness, then blinking as the moon appeared abruptly, flooding the scene with light.

There was a shadowy dappled form down at the pond, taking a drink of the clear water.

'Tikki –?' She stumbled forward, hoping he would not run away before she reached him. Surely, the rich succulent chicken would persuade him to stay by her side – at least until he finished it.

'Tikki –?' As she drew closer, the shadowy form grew larger, much larger than she had first thought. Too large to be a cat. Perhaps a fallen tree. Closer still, it looked an almost human shape. If she were superstitious, she might think she had somehow called the Centurion into being – or haunting – again. But it seemed more substantial than that ghostly presence. It was a solid shape, gaining definition as she advanced on it.

It *was* human! And female. Lying half-submerged at the edge of the water. Perhaps one of the paparazzi had stumbled in the darkness and fallen into the pond.

Stifling a scream, Margot flung aside the cup and dashed to help.

Help? Something about the motionless waterlogged form suggested that the woman was beyond help. Margot stooped for a closer inspection, trying to steel herself to pull the body out of the water or, at least, turn it over on its back.

As soon as she had done so, she realised her mistake. The woman was so obviously dead. Water drained away from the open eyes and parted lips, coursed off the front of the sodden suede jacket, the stiffening arms. There was no question of attempting any resuscitation technique. As for the kiss of life –

Retching, Margot backed away. She had seen enough to know that the woman was a stranger to her. What of the others in the house? Did one of them know her?

She had to tell someone. She backed farther away. She couldn't just leave the body lying here. She couldn't just turn and run, however much she wanted to.

The police! They would have to be called. A second dead woman found in the same garden! What would they make of that? They couldn't accuse Chloe this time; she was safely in their custody already. Perhaps she *was* innocent of the first murder, if a second had now been –

Murder? Where had that thought come from?

Darkness swooped at her, her knees threatened to buckle under her before she reached the house. How peaceful it would be to surrender consciousness and leave all the problems and decisions to someone else.

Who? Milly could not face the problems she already had. There would not be enough in the fridge to sustain Wilfred through this new crisis. And Nan . . . Nan was dangerously close to breaking down, as it was.

Emmeline! Emmeline, the tower of strength, with not

enough calls on that strength these days. She would tell Emmeline and let her handle everything.

Not even to herself did Margot want to admit the reason she did not consider rousing her cousins: the younger, stronger males in the family.

Not Richard, not Henry, not even Justin. So far as she could tell, from a quick look at her, the dead woman was of the right age to have been involved with any of them.

Chapter Fifteen

'But who is she?' Emmeline stared down at the body at her feet. 'And what is she doing here?'

'I thought you might recognise her,' Margot said.

'I don't know her.'

'I've never seen her before in my life.' Just to make sure, Emmeline bent down for a closer look. 'I'm sure, if she had ever been one of my pupils, I'd recognise her, no matter what state she was in, or however many years have passed.'

Margot had never thought of that. But how could Emmeline identify anyone who looked like that? One of Emmeline's past pupils? Seeking her out at home? For what reason? And why should she end up dead?

The police were on their way. Leave it to them.

They arrived without sirens and with a minimum of flashing blue lights.

Margot realised, as they conversed quietly with Emmeline, that a working relationship had long since been established. This was the second time around and they all knew the routine.

Quietly, one by one, Emmeline roused the others and the police spoke with them briefly. No one had seen or heard anything; no one had the slightest idea who the dead woman could be – or why she had died in their garden.

Briefest of all was the initial interview with Margot.

'She's ill and she's had a nasty shock,' Emmeline had warned the police, with more truth than she knew. Life had been nothing but a series of nasty shocks for a long time now, but how much did Emmeline know, or suspect, about her illness? Perhaps she had been over-optimistic to think she could conceal it from both the sharp eyes of a professional and those of a trained educationalist accustomed to dealing with adolescent girls and their myriad problems and neuroses.

The police, however, were not surprised that someone who had discovered a body should appear dazed and slightly disoriented. They had listened with apparent interest to her suggestion that the deceased might have been one of the paparazzi and assured her that they would look into that possibility – among others.

Just as she thought she might be on the point of fainting, they had ended the interview and allowed her to go back to her room.

But the peace and quiet she had been hoping to find was not there. The whole house seemed to be creaking and grumbling, resentful at its disturbed routine. Footsteps came and went, doors opened and closed on the ground floor. Outside, hushed voices rose and fell and lights flickered as the police went about their grim business.

The bedside clock said 3 a.m., so perhaps she was entitled to the exhaustion dragging her down. So much had happened, so deeply shocking and disturbing, it was not surprising that her nerves were frayed and complaining.

Despite her exhaustion, sleep eluded her. In the darkness, images of the events of the preceding hours seemed to swirl around her: the unknown woman, lying like a fallen tree, her dark brown trousers the trunk, her green and tan patchwork jacket the small leafy branches.

Then family faces crowded forward to haunt her, at first blurred and distorted, then sharpening into focus, but still disquieting, as she had last seen them, blinking and half-awake under the artificial lights downstairs.

136

Looking drawn and furtive, eyes shifting and avoiding all other eyes, they had tugged uneasily at rumpled night attire, obviously at a disadvantage against the fully clothed wide-awake representatives of the law.

Bewildered and innocent. Yes, they *had* to be innocent. Stunned by the second death in a year on their premises, they had huddled disbelievingly around the dining-room table, watching the police marching once again through their home, into their garden, in a nightmarish replay of the original situation.

At least, this time, Chloe was not – could not be – involved.

But a woman lay dead – and it was clear from the police attitude that they did not believe she had met with an accident.

Who, then, had killed her?

Because the woman had been young and attractive – so far as could be judged, making allowances for the inevitable changes wrought by death – the men of the family were the obvious suspects.

But Emmeline's reaction had shown that the women could not be ruled out entirely. She had not been one of Emmeline's pupils, but was it significant that Emmeline had not denied that she had been one of her former colleagues?

Or had she been an actress or someone in theatre that Christabel might have encountered – and grown to hate – in the course of her distinguished but chequered career?

Perhaps she had been one of the procession of au pairs who had worked in the house? But it was hard to imagine Milly, or even Nan, harbouring a grudge strong enough to explode into such drastic action.

Lynette . . .? Little Lynnie . . .? The only member of the household the police had shrunk from waking and questioning. Protected by her age and, possibly, by her father's position. Not to mention Nan, who had looked in on her and proclaimed that she was sleeping and should not be disturbed.

Lynette – there was that unthinkable thought again! But everything that had happened in this past terrible year was unthinkable.

The distorted images blurred again and retreated. The lights continued moving and flashing outside, the hum of voices went on relentlessly, but seemed to fade gradually into the distance.

Against the odds, she finally fell into an uneasy slumber.

Despite the fact that Aunt Milly was refusing to leave her room ('Not another one!' Emmeline said grimly), there was a livelier, more buoyant atmosphere at breakfast.

'They can't pin this one on Chloe!' Uncle Wilfred was close to something resembling his old jovial self. 'She's got the best alibi of any of us. She was locked up in Holloway – with a full roster of prison guards for witnesses!'

'It's sad about the poor dead girl,' Nan said. 'Terrible, really. But it isn't as if any of us knew her.'

'The police are going to need quite a lot of convincing on that score, I'm afraid.' Richard was taking a more sombre – or perhaps a more realistic – view. 'She was found in our garden, after all.'

'So much the better!' Wilfred speared another sausage and gnawed it thoughtfully. 'I don't want to sound callous but, if she had to go, she picked the best place for it. Throws the whole case against Chloe into disarray. With another corpse on their hands, the police will have to give her the benefit of some doubt.'

Margot began to feel an overwhelming sympathy for Aunt Milly. She wondered if it were too late to retreat into her own room and close the door against the world.

'Not really. It's just spreading the doubt around –' An uneasy stirring around the table silenced Christa abruptly. They had all picked up her as yet unvoiced thought:

If Chloe hadn't killed Claudia, then who had? Another corpse in the garden was reason enough to suspect that her killer might still be free – and still killing.

But who? And why?

Justin and Fenella were huddled as closely together as their chairs would allow. Their full attention appeared to be concentrated on their plates, but telltale side glances betrayed their discomfort. It was clear that they suspected everyone but each other. After all, they could prove they were out of the country at the time of the first murder.

And so could she. Margot crossed glances with Henry and looked away quickly. Where had he been then?

'Will we be going to court this morning?' Nan wondered. 'Will Chloe be there – after this?'

'Not for long,' Wilfred said. 'She'll have to appear, but it will just be a formality. I was on to Comfrey first thing this morning –'

'Dragged him out of bed at the crack of dawn,' Richard translated, not without pride in the renewed forcefulness of his father.

'Comfrey's certain they'll have to order an adjournment while the police investigate this new development –'

'They'll have to try to determine whether the two murders have any connection with each other.' Richard finished his coffee and pushed back his chair. 'Chloe is in with a fighting chance.'

'But she still isn't free.' Nan spoke sadly. 'Is she?'

'Not yet.' Wilfred pushed back his own chair and snatched a piece of Emmeline's buttered toast to take with him. 'But things are looking a lot better than they did yesterday.'

That depended on your point of view. Things certainly hadn't improved for the poor woman in the patchwork suede jacket who had been found head down in the pond.

'Mmmm . . .' Emmeline seemed to be thinking along the same line. 'Just remember, we aren't out of the woods yet.' Her sharp glance reminded them of more than that.

Richard was not the only male to twitch uneasily. Each of them was due for a further interview with the police. More probing questions would be asked – and not just about last night's mystery woman. The police would want to hark back to last year's murder and the precise nature of everyone's relations with Claudia.

And they might be right. Claudia had had her moods and, in the wrong mood, could be a bit of an emotional bully. Living by her emotions herself, she had sometimes delighted in pushing other people to the limits of theirs. Had she pushed someone too far?

'*So exciting!*' Claudia was back, the later Claudia. The young matron, mother and slightly bored political wife, acquiring new animation as she recounted her big adventure. '*Oh, that moment when they broke the door down and came storming into the room! Chills up and down my spine and goosebumps everywhere else! I'd never felt anything like it before. I thought I was going to die!*'

Only she hadn't, not there, not then. Nor in any other of the close brushes with eternity her subsequent travels had led her into. She had had to come home for that. Had she felt one last terrible burst of excitement as her attacker lunged at her with the knife?

Probably not. One of the damning points in the case against Chloe was the fact that there had been no defence wounds on Claudia's hands. She had trusted her attacker completely and the sudden assault had caught her unaware.

But that wouldn't have applied only to Chloe. Claudia would have trusted anyone in the family . . .

140

'. . . Margot?' Nan stood beside her, repeating her name. 'Margot, would you mind?'

'I'm sorry.' Margot turned to look at her, wrenched back to the present. 'I'm afraid I was miles away. Mind what?'

'Driving me to court this morning. I know nothing much is going to happen today but –'

Margot's heart twisted as she saw that Nan's hands had developed a slight tremor and she looked older, more haggard.

'But, if they adjourn the trial, it may be our last chance to see Chloe until . . . until heaven knows when.'

'Of course.' Margot saw that Wilfred and Richard had already departed while she had been deep in her own thoughts. 'Anyone else want to come along?'

'I think not,' Christa said. 'There's nothing we can do so –' She broke off, shrugging, her bracelets jangling as she reached for her coffee cup.

There was a murmur of agreement, perhaps tinged with relief, from the others.

'The fewer of us who show our faces today, the better.' Emmeline spoke with the voice of grim experience. 'The media will be back to doorstepping in force after this new development. Wrap a scarf around your faces, keep your heads down, your hand on the horn and don't stop for anything. If you hit one or two of them – good!'

Justin and Fenella exchanged a horrified glance. Emmeline had sounded as though she meant it.

Chapter Sixteen

Despite Emmeline's forebodings, they had no difficulty in getting away from the house.

As they drew near the Crown Court, however, increased numbers of media lurking outside told them that the first rumours of fresh news breaking had begun spreading.

'They know something's happening.' Margot drove past and, since it was morning and not a market day, managed to find a parking place nearby.

Nan took her arm as they hurried past the cameras and microphones, heads down, ignoring the shouts for attention.

'Just a word, please –'

'Is it true that –?'

'Over here! Look this way –'

'One minute – One minute –'

Then they were through the turmoil and up the steps and into the sanctuary of the courthouse. The last few dogged journalists trailing after them were restrained by the official at the security arch.

'In here –' Nan was looking frail and shaken. Margot led her into the lift and breathed a sigh of relief as the door closed and the glass-walled enclosure moved slowly up the atrium to the floor above.

There was a subdued bustle outside the courtroom, a rising sense of something about to happen. The media pool huddled together, staring avidly at every passer-by. The artist, sketchpad at the ready, was limning in light butterfly strokes outlining background, suggesting the tension and excitement of faceless figures leaning toward each other, expectant and eager . . .

'Keep moving,' Nan ordered, with a return to her old briskness, 'they've spotted us.'

Margot needed no urging. Her gaze had inadvertently crossed with that of the artist and she had seen the telltale twitch of his fingers as he swung to a blank corner of the page and began a new sketch. Of her.

'Just a minute . . . please . . .'

They evaded the notebook-clutching woman who had attempted to cut them off and hurried into the court-room.

'Sit at the end,' Nan directed unnecessarily. 'We may want to get away quickly.'

Her own opinion precisely. She and Nan firmly ensconced themselves. Opposite them, the jury filed into the jury box. Chloe was already in place, her head still bowed, her eyes still downcast.

The QCs were conspicuous by their absence, although their legal teams were at their benches, rather more alert than usual and with an air of expectancy.

The press box was overflowing, with some obvious media types spilling into the seats outside it. Clearly everyone was aware that something was about to happen. Everyone but the jury. And Chloe.

At the last minute, the QCs came bustling in and just had time to take their places before:

'*Court rise.*'

It seemed that they had barely reseated themselves when it was all over. The two QCs had advanced purposefully to the bench to confer briefly with the judge, who, obviously forewarned, seemed unsurprised at their representations.

'*Court adjourned.*'

There was a buzz of excitement. For the first time, Chloe lifted her head, startled. Comfrey QC hurried to her to impart the reason behind the adjournment.

In the stricken moment before Chloe lowered her head again, Margot saw the puzzlement – and the fear – in her eyes.

They ran into Verity as they left the building, pushing their way through the media throng, who were now undecided as to whether to accost them or head straight for a quote from Comfrey QC, who was always good value.

'What is it?' Verity was on her way in – or thought she was. She was obviously having second thoughts as she looked at the stream of people pouring out of the court-house. 'What's happened? Is it a bomb threat?'

'Adjournment.' Nan walked past without stopping, pulling Margot along with her.

'What? Why?' Verity pivoted in her tracks and followed them. 'What happened?'

'Doesn't Kingsley know?' It had not occurred to Margot that no one would have told Kingsley. On the other hand, why should they? Kingsley's position was anomalous, to say the least. He would not be the first person one of the family would rush to confide in.

'I haven't seen Kingsley this morning. He had to go back to London last night, he was expecting a vote in the House. He had to be there for it.' Verity didn't like admitting she had been left behind in The Roman Arms. Someone might notice that it was not the first time this had happened. In fact, Kingsley was making rather a habit of it. Margot wondered if there were someone else in London who was sharing those evenings when he had such important business in town. Undoubtedly, Verity was wondering the same thing.

'He'll sleep late after such a late vote,' Verity said defensively. 'He'll be here for the afternoon session . . . That is, he'd planned to be.'

'You can tell him he needn't bother,' Nan said. 'There

144

isn't going to be an afternoon session. The trial has been adjourned.'

'But why?' Verity demanded. 'What's going on?'

'It's something to do with new evidence the police will have to have time to investigate.' Margot was no more willing than Nan to go into specifics. Not with Verity.

'New evidence? How can there be? The case is a year old. They've had all the time in the world to find new evidence. Why wait until now? Kingsley is going to be very upset. He thought this nightmare was nearly over.'

'So did we all.' They were at the car, Nan wrenched the door open and dived inside. 'And now it's started all over again!' She slammed the door behind her.

'What? What?' Verity snatched at Margot's arm as she started to get into the driver's seat. 'What does she mean by that?'

'Verity, I can't go into it now.' Margot pulled away so sharply that Verity staggered back. 'Go home and turn your television on and find out!'

They hadn't told Lynette yet, either. Fortunately, she did not appear to have noticed that her television set had been unplugged and the batteries removed from her transistor radio. Emmeline's work, probably. A throwback to the precautions she had taken last year when Claudia's death had featured in all the newscasts. This would bring it all back. How long could they keep Lynette in ignorance of last night's events?

'Wrapping her in cotton wool again,' Christa snorted. 'What a shock it's going to be when that little madam finally has to go out and face the real world.'

'Trying to keep the peace a little while longer,' Emmeline corrected. 'There's enough chaos around here at the moment without having her start in, too.'

145

'She'll have to know sometime.' Christa almost seemed to relish the thought.

'Do you want to be the one to tell her?'

'Why should any of us have to tell her? Plug the television back in and let the evening news take the strain.' Christa had her practical side.

'She's being awfully quiet,' Henry said uneasily. 'It's most unlike her. Do you think she knows already?'

'I think Tikki is up there with her,' Emmeline said. 'I saw him slip into the house a little while ago. She's always quieter when she can play with him, he's a soothing influence.'

Listless and lethargic, Margot lay back in her chair, hearing conversation around her as from a great distance. She seemed to have expended her day's ration of energy in driving Nan to court and back. On their return, she had tossed her handbag down on the bed and stretched out beside it for as long as she dared before coming back downstairs to join the family conference.

Nan had taken over the kitchen to prepare a discreetly festive evening meal. It would not do to appear too jubilant in the light of another woman's demise, but Chloe's improved prospects surely deserved some celebration.

Uncle Wilfred and Richard were discussing those prospects even now with the legal team before they, too, adjourned and went back to their London chambers to await further reports of the police investigation and its implications for Chloe.

Aunt Milly was still in retreat, still reading with a desperate urgency that belied the expectations of the others. It was her garden Death had visited for a second time and, even though the victim was a stranger, she saw nothing to be cheerful about in the circumstance.

'. . . benefit may outweigh the awkwardness . . .' The conversation had moved on, but not by much. Margot stifled a yawn.

'. . . wonder who she was? What was she doing here when none of us knew her . . . or say we didn't.' As the only resident male present at the moment, poor Henry was on the defensive. 'I mean, it's not as though we live in a house fronting the High Street. We *are* off the beaten path. You can't just stroll into our garden to admire the flowers, you have to search us out. What did she want? Haven't the police found out who she is yet?'

'If they have, they aren't telling us,' Christa said. 'I suppose we couldn't expect them to.'

'Not until it suits their purpose,' Emmeline added grimly.

How many conversations like this had they had over the past year? Without the ray of hope now on the horizon. But also without the dark suspicion that a killer was still at large and might be one of them.

'Wasn't she carrying any identification . . .?'

'Of course, it's early days yet . . .'

The voices droned on soporifically; a delicious smell began wafting through the air from the kitchen. Slumped in the comfortable armchair, Margot felt her eyelids begin to droop. The last vestige of her attention drifted away and she abandoned the pretence that she was awake . . .

The first piercing scream from upstairs brought them all sitting bolt upright in their chairs.

'For God's sake!' Christa snapped. 'Isn't that damned bell good enough for her any more?'

There was another scream. And another.

'Lynette!' Nan came flying out of the kitchen. 'Lynette – what is it?'

The screams continued, rising in a crescendo of terror.

'Lynette!' Nan took the stairs at a breakneck pace, the others not far behind. 'It's all right, dear. We're coming!'

Tikki plunged down the stairs as the others rushed

up, nearly tripping them. His ears were laid back, his tail bristling.

'Did the cat scratch her?' Christa asked. 'Is that what this is all about?'

'Tikki doesn't scratch.' Henry's hand was firmly on the small of Margot's back, propelling her upwards – or keeping her from falling. Did he realise how weak she was?

'She's not in her room.' Nan came out more quickly than she had gone in and stood bewildered for a moment as the screams still resounded around them.

'I think she's in my room,' Margot said faintly, a cold dark foreboding settling over her.

'Your room?' Nan whirled about and dashed down the hallway. 'What's she doing there?'

From the way Lynette was screaming, Margot had a pretty good idea. This was not the first time the privacy of her room had been invaded by someone bored and lonely who amused herself by prying through other people's possessions. This time Lynette had found more than she had bargained for.

Margot moved to one side as the others crowded into the room and made straight for Lynette, still screaming and hysterical over by the window.

'Lynette, stop that!' Emmeline raised her hand just enough to emphasise that a good quick slap was the best remedy for hysteria, child abuse notwithstanding.

'There, there, dear.' Nan gathered Lynette into her arms. 'It's all right, dear, we're here.'

'But why is she here?' Christa voiced the pertinent question. 'I thought she never left her room.'

'So we all thought.' Emmeline's eyes were cold.

'Tikki . . . it was Tikki's fault.' The screams gave way to great gulping sobs. Lynette shrank back against Nan, frightened and defensive as she realised she had given herself away. 'Tikki made me follow him. He was frantic . . . he wanted . . .' She gestured helplessly.

The others followed the line of her gesture to see the

catnip mouse lying on the carpet where Tikki had abandoned it when her screams had frightened him away.

'It was his!' Lynette insisted. 'He told me it was. He . . . he could smell it, but he couldn't get it. He wanted me to take it out for him.'

Margot had forgotten all about that catnip mouse she had impulse-bought on market day. She had thrust it deep into her handbag and never given it another thought. There had been too much else to think about.

'I still don't understand.' Christa was giving no quarter. 'What are you doing in here? Where was it?' They stared at the mouse as though it could answer her questions.

But Margot knew where to look: at the handbag she had left lying on the bed, where Tikki must have jumped up and discovered it, sniffing out his treasure within. The bag was open now, with half its contents spread out across the counterpane, the sapphire-and-diamond earrings perilously close to the edge, in danger of slipping to the floor. The ear-rings had been in the small zippered compartment holding the key to –

The closet door was open, the suitcase dragged halfway into the room, the lid thrown back, its rumpled red-encrusted contents on display.

They had not been rumpled when she locked the case, nor had they been in a position to be easily displayed. The few items she had not unpacked had been neatly folded and arranged to conceal, from any casual observer, the parcel beneath.

The battered thick cardboard box, with its almost indecipherable address and its smattering of gaudy foreign stamps, had been tugged to the top and opened. The tattered garments within, stiff and unwieldy with dried blood, had been pulled out and then thrust back in horror as realisation dawned.

'Ask her!' From the refuge of Nan's arms, Lynette hurled her accusation:

'Ask Margot! Who has *she* killed?'

149

Chapter Seventeen

'Frankly,' Emmeline said, 'I'm relieved that it didn't turn out to be an infant corpse. Stillborn, or perhaps impulsively strangled in the throes of post-natal depression.'

Henry spilled some of the brandy he was pouring. Although inured to the riper comments of the females in the family, Emmeline's frankness could still jolt him. He gave a nervous apologetic smile and dabbed at the spilt liquid with his handkerchief.

'Happens all the time,' Christa said. 'Especially at airports – that's where they usually catch them. One is always reading about binned babies, or tiny bodies packed in the luggage. You were lucky to get away with it. If they'd ever searched your luggage, you'd have had some explaining to do.'

The expectant hush left no doubt that she still had some explaining to do.

'Nothing like that.' Margot felt her determined smile wavering. 'We weren't going to think about babies for a few more years. Not until we were married . . . until our photographic studio was established . . .' She gave up the struggle to hold on to the smile. 'Anyway, I'm far too conventional. Obviously, I was too well brought up.'

'Unlike Lynette,' Emmeline said, 'who is developing all of the earmarks of the school sneak.'

No one contested that opinion, but Nan was still upstairs trying to calm Lynette. Bemused expressions on their faces suggested that they might be remembering occasions when they had found things not quite as they thought they had left them in their own rooms. Had Lynette discovered any other secrets people had been trying to hide?

'You were saying . . .' Emmeline was not going to drop the subject. They had all seen the bloodstained clothing.

'Sven got a last-minute freelance assignment,' she forced the words out, 'covering a small uprising in the Far East. He was only supposed to be gone for a week. but . . . they took a wrong turning . . . their car was caught in the crossfire between the two factions. Sven and the UN observer were killed, the driver badly wounded. I was listed as Sven's next-of-kin, so they sent his belongings to me. There weren't many, he travelled light . . . the cameras . . . the carry-on bag with his other clothing . . . reached me eventually . . . a few weeks ago . . .' She leaned back and closed her eyes, wishing she could sleep for ever.

'And then . . . two days before I was due to leave to come over here . . . the rest of it . . . the last of it . . . arrived. I . . . I suppose they meant to be kind . . . or perhaps they didn't know what else to do with it. His wallet, with a picture of me and an old letter I had sent once . . . the money was missing, of course. I don't blame anyone for that . . . what does it matter? Perhaps they used it for the postage . . .'

She felt a glass nudge her hand and someone gently closed her hand around it. She opened her eyes and smiled gratefully at Henry.

'There was also his passport . . . and his credentials and . . . and the clothes he was wearing when . . .' She took a long swallow; it wasn't strong enough. It couldn't be. Nothing could ever be.

'I . . . I didn't know what to do with them . . . I was so shocked . . . and I didn't have time to think. So . . . so I . . .' Heads were nodding sympathetically. They knew what she had done.

'So . . .' She finished her drink and did not notice when Henry detached the glass from her hand to replenish it. 'So, I threw everything into my suitcase and brought it with me. I couldn't think what else to do. And it seemed so . . . so cold . . . just to leave them behind in an empty apartment.' No need to mention the other wild but persistent thought that had kept running through her head: perhaps she might be able to bury those . . . last remains . . . in a corner of the family plot, so that there would be a little bit of Sven, if only some of his blood, waiting there for her when her time came. So that she wouldn't have lost him completely.

'I'm sorry.' She took a deep swallow of her fresh drink. 'It was just unfortunate that Lynette should be the one to find them.'

'She wouldn't have found them if she hadn't been prying about where she had no business to be,' Emmeline said grimly.

'I *did* keep the suitcase locked,' Margot offered, in her own defence. '*And* at the very back of the closet.'

'Precisely!' Emmeline drained her own drink. 'We are going to have to have a very serious talk with that young lady in the morning.'

'Since she's now given herself away and we know that she can and does leave her room,' Henry spoke hopefully, 'Perhaps we can persuade her to move back into her old room. I know Uncle Wilfred would love to get his old quarters back.'

Ah, but would Aunt Milly? Emmeline and Christabel exchanged glances but, before anyone could say anything, Nan moved forward. How long had she been standing in the doorway listening?

'She's asleep now,' Nan reported. 'I had to give her one of her pills and sit with her until she dozed off. I think she'll sleep the night through now.'

'Asleep or not, she won't leave her room again tonight,' Christa said. 'She's been well and truly caught and she's smart enough to lie low for a while.'

'She's being over-optimistic if she thinks we'll forget about it.' Henry brought Nan a drink.

'She's been through so much,' Nan defended her chick. 'This must have thrown her right back to –'

'She brought it on herself,' Christa said sharply. 'And now she's been found out. Next time she dares to ring that damned bell, I hope you'll ignore it. I intend to!'

The quirk of Nan's lips suggested that that was all she had ever done, anyway. Emmeline sat watching quietly, a faintly absent look in her eyes betraying that she was absorbed in her own thoughts.

Her glass was becoming too heavy to hold, even though it was nearly empty again. Margot set it down on the floor beside her chair and leaned back again, closing her eyes against the overpowering weariness.

The sudden clang of the handbell ripped through the house, startling them. Margot found herself on the edge of her chair and she was not the only one.

'Oh, no!' Christa cried. 'No!'

'I'm sorry.' Nan pushed herself out of her chair so rapidly that she swayed for a moment before regaining her balance. 'I thought she was asleep.'

'Don't go!' Christa said. 'Stop humouring her!' But Nan was already out of the room.

Margot found herself on her own feet, propelled towards the doorway by a sudden panicked thought: *Where was Milly?*

'You're not going, too!' Christa said. 'I shouldn't think you'd ever want to see that brat again.'

'No, it's Milly,' she blurted out. 'All this uproar – and we haven't seen her –' *Hadn't anyone missed her?*

'Oh, Milly.' Christa gave an indifferent shrug. 'Don't worry about Milly. She's better off than we are. She's lost in her own little world.'

Perhaps, but Margot was going to make sure.

'Oh, hello, dear.' Milly looked up as she came into the morning room, now quite dark. The reading lamp was on, the usual open book in Milly's lap. 'Is dinner ready?'

'Almost.' Margot leaned against the door in relief. Milly was calm and unconcerned, showing no sign of having heard anything untoward. Why explain and upset her? 'We're having drinks in the library. Aren't you going to join us?'

'Oh, yes. In just a few more minutes, dear. Lady Philomena, in a fit of pique, is just about to hurl her engagement ring, the priceless Rosenthorpe diamond, over the edge of the abyss into the mountain cataract tumbling below, which will carry the ring out to sea, never to be seen again, thus unleashing the Rosenthorpe Curse on the entire dynasty.' Milly shook her head. 'These young girls – so impetuous . . .'

Margot backed out, closing the door silently behind her. It took her several moments to regain what passed for her composure before she returned to the library and accepted, wisely or unwisely, the fresh drink Henry immediately pressed into her hand.

No wonder none of the others had worried about Milly. They were used to it. She wondered whether she, too, would grow accustomed to the new unnerving Milly.

The ensuing long silence was neither uneasy nor companionable, just the silence of people who had nothing much to say to each other, but a lot to think about.

They looked up, with a rustle of expectation, as they heard Nan's footsteps coming down the stairs, then turn and move off down the hallway in the opposite direction. There was a clatter of pot lids being lifted and replaced, the slam of the oven door, the rattle of cutlery and concomitant sounds from the kitchen.

It seemed an eternity before Nan rejoined them to announce: 'Another half an hour.'

This was not really what they were interested in hearing.

'Well?' Christa demanded.

'She really is asleep now. I gave her another pill. I should have known she was so upset that one wouldn't be enough.'

'You should also know that that wasn't what I was asking,' Christa said severely. 'What did she have the nerve to want this time?'

'What does she ever want?' Nan sighed. 'She wants her mother, she wants her father, she wants her Aunt Chloe, she wants Tikki . . .' *She wants the world she lost.*

'Claudia and Chloe are impossible!' Christa said. 'She, of all people, should know that.'

'And after the way she frightened him away with her hysterics –' Emmeline paused while they all contemplated the memory of the terrified cat bolting down the stairs – 'I'd say it will be a long time before we see Tikki around here again.'

That left Kingsley.

Chapter Eighteen

'I really don't see why you need to bother Kingsley about every little tantrum.' Verity was determined to be the angel barring the way with a flaming sword. Either that, or she didn't like Lynette any better than Lynette liked her. 'He's very busy right now.'

'She's his daughter,' Nan reminded. 'His only child.'

'Yes . . .' *For the moment*, Verity's tone implied. She would be perfectly happy to see Kingsley walk away from his responsibilities, forget all about Lynette, about Claudia, about everything except starting a new life. With her. She, of course, would soon provide him with much more satisfactory progeny.

Did she have any idea just how unrealistic her ambitions were?

'It's all right.' Emmeline stood in the doorway. 'He's turned his cellphone back on and I've just spoken to him directly. He's promised he'll be down later this afternoon.'

'Well, really!' Verity huffed. '*I'm* supposed to make all his appointments for him.'

'I'm sure your employer –' Emmeline emphasised the word delicately and Verity's cheeks grew red – 'would not consider it necessary to make an appointment to see his own daughter when she needs him.'

'Well, really!'

Margot stepped aside as Verity stormed out of the room, then entered slowly and slumped into the nearest armchair. Above her head, the conversation went on.

'That girl is getting above herself,' Nan said.

'She has been for some time,' Emmeline agreed. 'It won't be doing Kingsley any good if she treats his constituents that way.'

'She's just two-faced enough to be perfectly charming to them,' Nan said. 'But eventually they'll see through her.'

But would Kingsley?

'Was it very bad?' Margot opened her eyes to find Nan standing over her.

'Probably not. It's just that they go on and on so.' Her longer, more searching interview by the police had just been concluded. 'Richard is in there with them now.'

'Boring and exhausting,' Emmeline concurred. 'They questioned me first thing this morning and I thought I'd never get away, even though I had nothing to tell them.'

'Nor I,' Nan agreed. 'They still seem to have no idea who the woman was. I don't see how they can get very far unless they know her identity.'

'They know she's dead,' Emmeline said harshly. 'That's enough to be getting on with.'

'They're still trying to establish a link with someone in this house.' Nan ran her fingers through her hair despairingly. 'They'll never be able to. Wherever she came from, whatever she wanted – it can't have had anything to do with us.'

'Then why was she here?' Emmeline asked.

'Perhaps . . . she was meeting someone here,' Margot said slowly. 'From one of the other houses in the area. We have the most extensive grounds around, with lots of little nooks and crannies where people could meet unseen.'

'It's landscaped better than the estates in some of Milly's Regency romances,' Nan agreed reflectively. 'Just laid out for assignations: the rose arbour, the herb garden, the gazebo . . .' Her voice faltered. '. . . the pond.'

'And Lynette told me –' A memory surfaced at the back of Margot's mind. 'There's been a prowler in the garden recently.'

'What?' Nan tensed. 'When?'

'A couple of days ago. I looked out of her window when she complained about it, but I couldn't see anyone. That's not to say no one was there, with so much shrubbery, so many shadows, they could have been hiding anywhere.'

Nan and Emmeline exchanged glances.

'Hasn't Lynette mentioned it? I thought that was what she was so anxious to tell Nan.'

'I hope you didn't tell the police about this,' Emmeline said.

'No, I've just remembered it now.' There had been so much else to think about that one more of Lynette's bids for attention was easily forgotten.

'That's good.' Nan relaxed. 'We don't want them harassing Lynette again. She's had enough to deal with.'

So have I. Margot felt her eyes closing again and did not fight against it.

'Two strangers roaming about the grounds . . .' Emmeline tested the idea thoughtfully. 'Choosing to meet each other here . . . it seems unlikely.'

Perhaps only one of them was a stranger.

'I don't know . . .' Nan was equally thoughtful. 'Meeting on neutral territory, as it were . . . especially if they had a score to settle.'

'And where better to kill someone than a garden where a previous killing had taken place?' Emmeline was warming to the idea. 'Shift the blame and suspicion to people who are already under suspicion.'

But were they? With Chloe in jail and on trial, surely the police would not have continued to suspect anyone else. Until this had happened.

'The main thing,' Nan said, as though she and Emmeline had been conducting another conversation

158

beneath the obvious one, 'is to keep Lynette well away from the police. She seems to be under control now but, under questioning, who knows what she might blurt out?'

Margot opened her eyes to find them both regarding her. With sympathy, with concern and, yes, with suspicion. Her explanation for the bloodstained garments concealed in her luggage had been the truth – but had they really believed her?

Belief or not, they were right. If Lynette were to tell the police what she had found . . . asked again, '*Who did she kill?*' . . . then the full force of the investigation would be centred on Margot.

And she couldn't blame them. Two murders did not necessarily mean that the same person must have committed both. Not when there was another hot suspect to hand. Better than anyone else, the police knew about criminal families: shoplifting rings, drug dealing, car stealing, burglary and handling stolen property, all as much group activities in certain circles as landscaping the garden or redecorating the house were in normal families. It would not be outside the range of possibilities for the police to consider that homicide might also run in families.

And she was one of the family. One, moreover, who travelled with bloodied clothing in her suitcase. The police would probably contact their colleagues in New York to find out whether any of her friends or acquaintances had been murdered lately.

If they could pin this murder on her, then Chloe still wouldn't be free.

Chloe's trial would resume and, later, there would be another, separate, trial – for her.

She was aware of Emmeline and Nan watching her silently. Had they come to the same conclusion?

'There's no reason for the police to question Lynette at all,' Nan said firmly. 'The woman was killed at the pond. On the other side of the house, at the far end of

the garden. Lynette couldn't possibly have seen anything from her window, even if she ever went near her
window. And the police know the situation, they've
known it all along. They know she never leaves her
room.'

Oh, doesn't she? The rest of them knew different now,
but it would be better if the police didn't find out. Better
for all of them.

Especially since it was clear that last night was not the
first time Lynette had left that room. Margot remembered the day she had found her ear-ring on the floor,
her belongings disturbed. Had Lynette regarded the
locked suitcase as a personal affront? Or a challenge.
How long had Lynette been in the habit of prowling –
sneaking – about the house, prying into other people's
belongings when she thought there was no one around
to catch her?

The house and . . . possibly . . . the grounds?

'It might not be a bad idea,' Emmeline said thoughtfully, 'if Kingsley were to take Lynette back to London
with him for a few days.'

And wouldn't Verity love that? And, now that she came
to think of it, where was Verity? Verity had flounced out
of the room some while ago, but there had been no slam
of the front door to denote that she had left the
house.

'Yes,' Nan sighed. 'That might be best. If she'll go . . .
If he'll take her . . .'

'Where did Verity go?' Margot asked abruptly.

'Ah, yes, Verity.' They both nodded, as though she
had scored a major point.

'Verity will still be around here somewhere,' Nan said.
'She always is when there's trouble.'

'Holding a watching brief for Kingsley,' Emmeline
confirmed.

Again there was a long exchange of glances.

'She won't have gone far.' Nan started for the door.
'Perhaps I ought to go and see . . .'

'Bloody woman!' Richard appeared in the doorway, blocking her exit. 'I nearly knocked her over. She was outside the door, listening! She scuttled off before I could grab her! Who does she think she is? Who let her in, anyway?' It was not difficult to know who he meant.

'We didn't let her in.' Emmeline looked as though she had just realised that. 'Of course, Kingsley had Claudia's key. He must have had a duplicate made for Verity.'

Or Verity had taken care of that little matter for herself.

'Then it's high time we changed the locks!' Richard fumed. That, too, was not a bad idea.

'How did the interview go, dear?' Nan tried to be soothing, but it was the wrong question.

'Go? Go? How should it go? They hammered away at me endlessly, obviously hoping I'd break down and confess, despite the fact that I have nothing to confess. I'd never seen the bloody woman in my life.'

'None of us had,' Emmeline said.

'I suppose the only thing to be grateful for is that the autopsy proved that the damned creature wasn't pregnant! If she had been, they'd really have had an excuse to pull out all the stops. DNA tests all around, I shouldn't wonder – and leaks to the media, for good measure.'

'But she wasn't,' Emmeline said, with more certainty than was actually reassuring. She sounded as though she might have been able to tell the police that before the autopsy.

'No, no . . .' Richard's indignation began to abate, replaced by a puzzled expression. 'In fact, they didn't seem terribly interested in the possibility. What they really want to know is why she was wearing a Kevlar vest under her jacket.'

'What kind of vest?' Nan's brow wrinkled. That was a new trade name to her.

161

'Kevlar.' Richard elucidated: 'The police want to know why someone visiting this house should have felt it necessary to wear a bulletproof vest.' He frowned.

'For that matter, I'd rather like to know the answer to that myself.'

Chapter Nineteen

'Whoever she was, she must have been expecting trouble,' Emmeline said.

'Which proves she must have been on her way to, or from, somewhere else,' Richard insisted. 'No one in this house has ever owned a gun.'

'She wasn't to know that, was she?' Henry countered. 'In any case, she wasn't shot, she was drowned.'

In deference to Aunt Milly's presence, the conversation had been suspended during lunch. Now that Milly had gone back to the morning room, the others had returned to their speculation with renewed zest.

'I suppose it couldn't have been a mugging in the town that went wrong?' Even Nan was joining in. 'And they decided to dispose of the body in our grounds?'

'Hell of a long way to cart a body!' Christa disposed of that theory briskly. 'And she was drowned, remember. In our pond.'

'I should have had that pond filled in long ago.' Uncle Wilfred was in breast-beating mood. 'It was never safe with all the children around.' He began searching frantically through his pockets.

'But none of them ever came to any harm,' Nan reminded him. 'Only this . . . stranger.'

'A stranger – does that make it any better? The woman is still dead.' Belated guilt was catching up with Uncle Wilfred. He was no longer thinking only of the advantage to Chloe. He found a stray mint, fuzzy with lint, and popped it into his mouth. 'Dead – in our garden. How could it have happened?'

Only too easily. Obviously. The real question was why it had happened. And also, to whom?

'There must be some way to speed up the police procedures,' Margot said tentatively. 'Can't Mr Comfrey chivvy them along? With all the computers and internet connections they have access to these days . . .' She trailed off. The others were looking at her incredulously.

'Are you mad?' Christa was plainly speaking for them all. 'We want as little to do with the police as possible. And don't think they'll jump to attention just because the Great Comfrey snaps his fingers. Quite the contrary, it would only antagonise them.'

'Let them get on with it in their own way,' Richard agreed.

'And without us!' Christa was determined about that.

'It was just a thought.' Thoroughly squelched, Margot withdrew from the conversation. Perhaps she *was* mad. Little side glances aimed at her when they thought she wasn't looking betrayed uncertainty.

But then, Justin and Fenella were always darting little side glances at everyone. They would be glad to get back to the clean and honest cut-throat world of show business and away from the dangers inherent in family life.

In this family, anyway. Margot closed her eyes, too tired to think. *Or too afraid?* Another thought she did not have the energy to explore. *Or the courage?*

The doorbell chimed, an unexpected – and unfamiliar – sound. They didn't have many visitors these days.

'The police are back?' Nan looked dismayed.

'I shouldn't think so,' Richard said. 'I had the distinct impression that they were through with us for the day when they finished questioning me this morning. I saw them out myself.'

The doorbell chimed again.

'I'll go,' Margot said, since everyone else seemed so reluctant.

'Margot!' Kingsley stood there. And Verity, of course. 'How well you look.' He stepped in and brushed her cheek with his lips. Verity sniffed.

'I'm sorry I couldn't get here earlier,' Kingsley said, 'but I talked to Lynette on the telephone and she understands.'

Margot nodded, half-listening for the imperious summons of the handbell from upstairs, but there was only silence. That must have been quite some talk Emmeline had had with Lynette this morning. Or perhaps Nan had administered another pill or two, strictly in the interests of keeping the peace – especially with the police present. It would not have done to call Lynette to their attention.

'I think she might be asleep –' Margot broke off. Kingsley was already heading for the stairs, Verity trailing reluctantly after him.

'Who is it?' The doorbell chimes had done what all other commotion could not and drawn Milly out of her refuge. She looked around eagerly – who did she hope to see? – and her face fell when she saw it was only Kingsley.

'Milly!' He strode forward and bestowed a double kiss, once on each cheek. 'How are you?'

'All right.' Milly seemed to brace herself against further onslaughts, her gaze still turned hopefully towards the front door. 'Are you alone?'

'*I'm* with him.' Verity issued the words like a challenge.

'Oh . . . yes.' Aunt Milly averted her gaze and began to retreat.

'Wait!' Kingsley said. 'Don't go! I've brought you a present.' He fumbled with the latch on his briefcase and wrenched it open, pulling out a large book. 'A bio-

165

graphy!' he announced triumphantly. 'Of a real Regency character –'

'Real? Oh, no!' Aunt Milly pressed the book back into his hands. 'Oh, no, dear. Thank you, but no. I never read biographies. Emmeline tried to give me some, but I had to make her understand. You see, you read them and you get so fond of the people and then . . . they die . . .'

'They die . . .' Milly took one final step and closed the door behind her, her words echoing forlornly through the hall.

'I – I thought –' Kingsley stared after her blankly, clutching his disdained offering. 'I thought she'd be pleased.'

'She isn't herself,' Verity said quickly. 'You know that.'

'I brought a present for Lynette, too.' He turned uncertainly to Margot. 'That's why I wasn't here earlier. I stopped to do some shopping along the way.'

'You should have let me do the shopping,' Verity said. 'I told you that.'

'A jigsaw puzzle. Do you think she'll like it?' Ignoring Verity, he was still seeking Margot's approval.

'I think she'd like to go back to London with you,' Margot said. 'At least, for a few days.'

'That's out of the question!' Verity answered for him. 'We have far too much to do to be able to cope with an invalid, as well. There's nobody there to wait on her all day.'

'Actually, Verity's right.' Kingsley was apologetic. 'Lynette is much better off here. She'd find London too upsetting.'

More upsetting than a place where they kept finding dead bodies in the garden? Margot doubted that.

'I know,' Kingsley said, as though she had spoken the thought. 'But she'd be bored and lonely. Very lonely, with no one around all day. It suits her here.'

Or, more accurately, it suited Kingsley. As it had

166

suited Claudia. Why had they bothered to have a child at all? Was it just to complete the picture of the perfect political family? To please the voters? To provide good picture fodder?

'She *is* all right?' Kingsley's anxious eyes met Margot's. 'At least, she's no worse?'

He did care. And probably Claudia had, too. It was just that a child had cramped their style and it was so convenient, when Milly maintained what amounted to a family nursery, to simply leave the child there and go off about their more exciting concerns. They knew Lynette would have the best of care, Milly was ever-welcoming, so where was the harm?

'I think Lynette is . . . very disturbed,' Margot said. No need to tell him why.

He nodded and started again for the stairs, then hesitated. 'Are you coming up?'

'I'd better not.' The sight of her might start Lynette off again. 'You're the one she wants to see.'

'Yes.' He looked as though he had been summoned to a particularly unpleasant interview with the Prime Minister.

'Alone,' Margot added, as Verity started after him.

'She's right.' Kingsley dismissed Verity. 'You stay down here. I won't be long.'

Verity's eyes flashed, but she turned meekly and followed Margot into the library. The others looked up, regarding Margot as they might have regarded Tikki dragging in something especially unsavoury. Even Verity seemed to notice a certain lack of warmth and feel that she had to overcome it.

'Kingsley has gone up to Lynette!' Verity announced, as triumphantly as though she had personally engineered it.

'I should hope so.' Nan gave her an old-fashioned look.

'Well, he's frightfully busy right now,' Verity defended. 'He has all that lost time to make up. It's lucky the trial was adjourned, it was throwing him way off schedule.'

Another one with a curiously skewed definition of lucky. Margot closed her eyes and found that she didn't feel quite so tired when she didn't have to look at Verity – it was bad enough to have to listen to her.

'. . . and, perhaps I shouldn't be telling you this, but you *are* family –' Even more triumph throbbed in Verity's voice. 'This is not for general information yet but – it's pretty certain that Kingsley is going to be offered a Cabinet post in the next reshuffle!'

The murmur of approval managed to sound interested, if not wildly enthusiastic.

'That's good news.' Richard sounded as though he might be calculating how this information could be used to best advantage.

How thrilled Claudia would have been. The culmination of all her ambitions for Kingsley. Well, perhaps not the absolute culmination: only the position of Prime Minister would have sufficed for that. But it was a giant step in the right direction.

'Are we boring you?' Verity demanded sharply.

'Sorry –' Margot had no doubt that the question was aimed at her. 'I'm afraid jet lag strikes again.'

'Does it?' Verity jeered. 'You have the longest case I've ever heard of. Perhaps you should try for the Guinness Book of Records.'

The atmosphere, as everyone avoided looking directly at Margot, told her that Verity was not the only person who had had that thought.

'That's enough, Verity.' Emmeline called her to order. 'Margot has been ill.'

How did she know that?

'Very ill,' Nan confirmed.

Had no one been deceived?

'Oh, I'm so sorry.' The gloating look Verity turned on Margot said that it couldn't have happened to a better person. 'I had no idea.'

'There's no reason why you should.' *Even Christa had known.* 'It's nothing to do with you.'

'Oh, but, if she's here with Lynette – helping take care of her . . .'

'It's nothing contagious,' Margot assured her. 'I'm just very, very tired. And sometimes very weak.' That was as specific as she cared to get. The others were way ahead of her.

'ME!' Verity cried, with barely subdued glee. 'Myalgic encephalomyelitis! People with that can't do anything at all. No wonder you're not running around with your camera, photographing everything in sight, the way you used to!'

'That's right, you haven't really been your old self since you got here.' Nan spoke as though a lot of things were becoming clear to her.

'Chronic Fatigue Syndrome,' Christa said. 'A lot of people in the theatre have it – and are doing some of their finest acting trying to prove that they haven't.'

'I think . . .' Uncle Wilfred had begun to twitch and, after searching frantically through every pocket, lurched to his feet. 'I think there was some lemon curd tart left over . . .' With obvious relief, he left the women to their discussion of ailments and headed for the fridge.

'Post Viral Fatigue,' Emmeline diagnosed. 'I should have spotted it myself. Heaven knows I've seen enough of it at school.'

Margot leaned back and closed her eyes again. A faint ringing in her ears and a feeling of dizziness warned her that it would not be wise to stand up now, however much she wanted to escape the room.

'TATT!' Nan declared. '"Tired All The Time", that's what the doctors call it. There's so much of it around that it has its own acronym.'

'Yuppie flu – there's a positive epidemic,' Richard confirmed. 'Especially in the City after a heavy weekend.' This levity brought him disapproving looks from the others.

In the distance, a telephone began ringing. They listened as Uncle Wilfred's footsteps diverted from the direction of the kitchen as he went to answer it.

'Oooh . . . but should we be keeping you up like this?' Verity oozed false sympathy. 'Wouldn't you rather go upstairs and lie down –?' Then she seemed to recollect who else was upstairs and changed tack abruptly. 'Or perhaps you could stretch out on the chaise-longue in the morning room. I'm sure Aunt Milly wouldn't mind.'

'I'm quite all right, thank you.' Margot opened her eyes and forced herself upright, fighting a fresh surge of dizziness. She would not show weakness in front of Verity.

'Oh, but you don't look it. Are you –?'

'That was Henry. He'll be home soon,' Uncle Wilfred reported from the doorway, looking puzzled. 'He stopped off at the police station for his interview on the way. He says they've identified that woman now. Someone called Polly Parsons. Never heard of her.'

Blank looks and shaking heads affirmed that no one else had, either.

'Some sort of travel agent, it seems. Ran her own company. Pop Tours. Never heard of them, either.'

'Pop Tours? You mean raves and rock concerts and that sort of thing?' Emmeline looked down her nose.

'It doesn't sound like anything any of us would know about,' Nan said.

'Polly Parsons of Pop?' Christa was openly incredulous. 'The police had better get back to the old drawing board and find out her real name. That one's a phoney, if I ever heard one.'

There was a choking gasp from somewhere in the room and the thud of a body hitting the carpet. They all turned to stare down at it in amazement.

Margot might have been feeling excessively weak – but it was Verity who had fainted.

Chapter Twenty

'What's the matter with her?' Uncle Wilfred demanded, stepping back nervously. 'She's not . . .?' He couldn't bring himself to say the word.

'Just fainted.' Nan crouched beside Verity, expertly checking her pulse.

'Perhaps Kingsley has been working her too hard?' Christa speculated. 'One way or another.'

Margot studied Verity thoughtfully before deciding that the faint was genuine. Verity had landed too heavily and in too ungraceful a position for it to have been calculated.

'Are you going to leave her there?' Uncle Wilfred stared down unhappily at yet another female body prone on his premises. 'Aren't you going to pick her up?'

'Must we?' Christa murmured.

The others seemed to be of the same mind; no one rushed forward to help Verity to her feet. In fact, it was rather peaceful to have her out of the picture, just lying there, quiet for once.

'Let her recover first.' Nan straightened up. 'Someone get a glass of water.'

'To throw over her?' Richard was hopeful.

'For her to drink. She'll be thirsty when she comes to.'

'I don't know . . . I don't know . . .' Shaking his head, Uncle Wilfred retreated kitchenwards.

'Dad . . .?' Richard followed, obviously not trusting

his father to carry out the errand, a mistrust confirmed by the eventual faint sounds of someone foraging through the fridge.

'Digging his grave with his teeth,' Nan sighed.

'He'll be all right when Chloe comes home,' Christa said.

Would he? Chloe's return wouldn't alter the fact that Claudia was gone for ever.

'What's going on here?' Kingsley was back. 'What's happened to Verity?'

'Nothing,' Nan said. 'She just fainted.'

'But . . . why?'

A faint stirring at his feet and a long moan answered him.

'She's coming round.' Nan stated the obvious.

'Here's the water.' Richard elbowed Kingsley out of the way and handed the glass to Nan. 'You're sure –?' Wistfully, he pantomimed a quick deluge for Verity.

'Thank you, dear.' Nan took the glass firmly.

'Ooooooh . . .' Verity's eyes fluttered open to an obviously unnerving view of human ankles and furniture legs. 'Where am I?'

'Verity!' Kingsley dashed forward to help as she struggled to sit up. 'Are you all right?'

'I . . . think so.' She leaned against him, in no hurry now to get up. 'What happened?'

'You fainted,' Nan said briskly, holding out the glass of water. 'Drink this.'

'Here . . .' Kingsley took the glass and held it to Verity's lips, echoing Nan's command. 'Drink this.'

'Yes.' Verity took a dainty sip, then suddenly gulped it down greedily as she discovered just how thirsty she was.

'Better?' Kingsley was frowning at her anxiously. Perhaps Verity had reason to be complacent, after all.

'How's Lynette?' Emmeline looked at Kingsley coldly. 'Does *she* feel better now?'

'Lynette will be all right.' Kingsley spoke with a trace

172

of irritation. 'Naturally, she's still a bit upset. This house hasn't been the most peaceful spot on earth of late.'

Margot braced herself to meet his accusing gaze, but he was looking off into space a trifle abstractedly. Was it possible that Lynette had not told him what she had found in Margot's room? Of course, to do so would have been to admit her own duplicity – and Lynette valued her father's high opinion of her.

'All right . . . easy now . . .' Kingsley was lifting Verity to her feet. 'Over here . . .' He guided her, leaning heavily on his arm, to an empty chair.

The others watched in silence as Kingsley fussed over Verity. Margot was vaguely aware of the front door opening and closing.

'Well, Henry?' If he'd hoped to slip into the room quietly, he had reckoned without Emmeline. 'Did you manage to convince the police that you hadn't taken in any rock concerts recently?'

'What?' Henry looked at her blankly. 'Rock? Me? Where did you get that idea?'

'Pop Tours,' Richard said. 'You told Dad they found out the dead woman owned and ran Pop Tours.'

'Oh.' Henry's face cleared. 'No, not that kind of pop, nothing to do with music at all. It was a small specialist travel agency. PoP stands for Places of Peril . . . very specialist, indeed.'

'Lean over and put your head between your knees, Verity,' Emmeline advised. 'We don't want you fainting again.'

'I'm all right.' Verity raised her head and gave Emmeline a hostile look. 'But –' she turned her paper-white face towards Kingsley and forced her pale lips into a smile – 'I'd like more water, please.'

'Yes, of course.' Kingsley took the glass and looked around for someone else to hand it to. No volunteers rushed forward – he was not at his office now.

'Specialist travel,' Richard said. 'Places of Peril sounds very specialist.'

173

'I didn't know there were travel agencies like that,' Henry said wonderingly. 'I mean, I realised there were agencies who'd tailor tours to special requirements, but I thought that meant handicapped people, wheelchair access, that sort of thing. Or special interests like archaeology, gardens, museums, opera houses . . .'

'Places of Peril,' Emmeline said thoughtfully. 'Does that mean what I think it means?'

'Precisely. The lady ran tours to the flashpoints of the world – and she wasn't the only tour operator who did.' Henry had learned too much too fast, more than he had ever wanted to know. 'If revolution threatened, if insurgents lurked behind every bush, if terrorists were hurling home-made bombs, if kidnapping, anarchy, ethnic cleansing were rife, PoP would be there – escorting a small, but select, tour.'

'Well, that explains the bulletproof vest,' Christa said. 'It's not usually part of your average woman's wardrobe.'

It also explained why Margot had briefly mistaken the body for a fallen tree. The patchwork jacket in greens and browns, the dark trousers, were a deliberately stylised camouflage outfit, designed to ensure that its wearer blended into the foliage in the country, but modish enough to pass unremarked in the city.

'I don't understand,' Nan said faintly. 'What sort of people would want to go to places like that?'

'There are more of them than you'd think. People who crave excitement: the danger junkies, the fright groupies, the thrill seekers. People who get a charge out of walking a tightrope, laying their lives on the line.' Henry paused.

'Sound like anyone we knew?'

Claudia!

Margot looked around at the others. Had they made the connection yet? More importantly, had the police?

Verity gasped and sagged against Kingsley. Just at that moment, he looked up and met Margot's eyes.

'Help me get Verity into the garden,' he said. 'She needs air.'

Automatically, she went to him while Henry still held the attention of the others. Verity was almost a dead weight, barely able to take a few steps as they half-dragged her along.

'All very discreet . . .' Henry was saying behind them. 'Word of mouth recommendations and no advertising. They hid the name of the agency behind the initials and no one was the wiser. If the occasional pop music fan tried to make a booking for a concert, they simply said there were no places left . . .'

'I didn't know,' Verity gasped as the cool air hit her. 'I didn't know.'

'I had no idea.' Kingsley, too, was distancing himself at a rate of knots. 'Verity always took care of the travel arrangements. And, of course, Claudia went on trips by herself when the House was in session and I couldn't get away.'

'Claudia gave me the name of the agency,' Verity said. 'She told me they might be expensive, but they were the best. She . . . she was always very satisfied with them.'

Henry's voice faded as Kingsley led them around the corner of the house to the lawn in front of the rose arbour where the cluster of white-painted iron garden benches and chairs waited in the last of the late afternoon sun. As they neared, the round tawny cushion in one corner of a bench moved and raised an enquiring head to watch their approach.

'Hello, Tikki.' Margot sat down beside him while he wriggled about amiably to accommodate her. She stroked the soft fur, with the relieved feeling that she had found a friend to provide a bit of moral support.

Verity and Kingsley had seated themselves side by side on the opposite bench, both looking extremely thoughtful. The silence lengthened.

'Polly . . . I can't believe it,' Verity said at last. 'Why didn't someone tell me?'

'They've only just found out,' Margot said. 'And you weren't here when we found her. The police wouldn't have thought of asking you if you could identify her.'

How could they be sure Verity hadn't been here? She had her own key to the house, to come and go as she pleased, ostensibly as Kingsley's emissary. She could have come back to the house after dark, when everyone was in bed, to meet the travel agent who, given her background, would not think such an assignation too unusual – although she had taken the precaution of wearing her Kevlar vest.

Verity, who had made such headway with Kingsley since Claudia's death. Verity, who had handled all the travel arrangements, who had known Polly Parsons. *Verity . . .?*

Tikki changed his mind about moulding himself along her thigh and moved into her lap instead. Margot stroked the sun-warmed fur, felt the heated iron floral design of the bench gently brand itself into her back and let her eyes close for a moment. Tikki had the right idea. How lovely it would be to doze in the warmth until the sun dipped below the horizon and then go into the house for a delicious hot dinner before going upstairs for a long refreshing sleep until morning.

'Do you think . . .?' Verity sounded almost timid. 'Could Polly have killed Claudia? If Chloe didn't do it, that is.'

'She didn't.' Kingsley was now prepared to give Chloe a vote of confidence.

'Why should she?' Margot asked. *And, even if she had, then who had killed her?*

Suddenly, she did not feel comfortable sitting so near to Verity with her eyes closed.

Verity, who'd had everything to gain by disposing of Claudia. But why on earth would she want to kill the travel agent?

Why should anyone want to kill a travel agent? If their trip had not been satisfactory, people demanded their money back, complained to ABTA, in extreme cases, even sued. They did not resort to murder.

In any case, Claudia had told everyone that her last trip had been the best of her life. There had been no hint of discontent. But Claudia was dead . . .

Margot opened her eyes to find Kingsley and Verity watching her. Disconcerted, she stopped stroking Tikki for a moment and he mewled a protest, a surprisingly kittenish sound for so adult a cat.

'Sorry, Tikki.' Margot resumed stroking him. His purring was loud in the uneasy silence. He was heavy, pinning her down, precious seconds might be lost in dislodging him if she should have to run for her life.

Where had that thought come from? She blinked and the sense of menace faded. Kingsley and Verity became again just two people she had known for most of her life, practically members of the family. Kingsley, certainly, by marriage; Verity, because she had always been around.

'Are you feeling better?' Margot asked her abruptly.

'What?' Verity was startled; she seemed to have forgotten that they were all sitting there because she had fainted. 'Oh! Oh, yes. Much better.' She didn't look it.

'Do you want to go back to the hotel?' Kingsley seemed of the same opinion. 'I shan't need you any more tonight.'

'No, no.' That was what she was afraid of. 'I'm quite all right now. Really, I am. It was just . . . a passing weakness.' She bared her teeth at Margot. 'You should know all about that. Except that yours doesn't pass, does it?'

'You're obviously feeling better,' Kingsley said drily. So he was not unaware of Verity's bitchy streak. But did he realise how deep it went, how deadly she might be?

'Perhaps I'm not quite as well as I ought to be.' Verity

covered her tracks quickly. 'But you were right –' She smiled adoringly at Kingsley. 'I do feel much better for being out in the nice fresh air.'

'Yes.' Margot also smiled at Kingsley, a more genuine smile. 'It's so lovely out here in the garden. We should make more use of –' The reason why they didn't returned to choke her off.

'That will come,' Kingsley said comfortingly.

Would it? Now that there had been a second unresolved death here? It seemed unlikely.

And yet, this was the family garden, the family home. She could not see Uncle Wilfred selling up and moving away. He and Aunt Milly had always loved the place so much, they were so deeply rooted here. Where would they go?

Margot shivered. The sun had gone down and the autumn chill in the air was making itself felt. A sharp gust of wind scattered petals from the dying roses over them, some hitting her cheeks then falling on Tikki in her lap.

'The last rose of summer . . .' Kingsley caught one of the petals, rubbing it thoughtfully between his fingers.

'Why can't this be over?' Verity burst out. 'Why can't everyone leave us alone and everything go back to being the way it was?'

'Because two women are dead,' Margot said. 'Murdered.' Nothing was ever going to be the same again.

'That's silly!' Verity said. 'They were accidents. Chloe got into a fight with Claudia and hit her, forgetting that she was holding a knife. It was just bad luck that she hit a vital spot and Claudia died. And that travel woman, prowling around where she had no right to be, tripped and fell into the pond and drowned.'

Was that what had happened? It sounded almost plausible. Especially if you substituted the name Verity for Chloe in the first instance. It was only too easy to imagine Verity, jealous and goaded beyond endurance, flying at Claudia with a knife she had 'forgotten'.

178

What about 'that travel woman'? Verity handled all the travel arrangements, Kingsley had said. And Verity had been quick to point out that the agency had been very expensive. Had Claudia and Kingsley been too trusting, leaving arrangements – and payments – to Verity? Had Verity been inflating invoices and skimming off the extra for herself? Or had she been cheating Polly Parsons in some way? And had the travel agent found out and arrived to expose her?

Or had she been discovered earlier, by Claudia, who had made the mistake of confronting her before telling Kingsley about it? Verity would not have hesitated to kill to keep Kingsley from knowing.

Had Verity killed Claudia, not in an insane burst of jealousy, but just to cover up a bit of common ordinary larceny? Could it be as simple as that?

'. . . Verity? . . . Margot?' Nan's voice could be heard calling, coming closer. 'Ah – here you are.' She came into sight and advanced on Verity. 'I've brought you your water.'

'Oh,' Verity said flatly. 'How kind.' By this time, she had forgotten she had ever asked for it. 'You shouldn't have bothered.'

'No bother at all.' Nan held the glass out to her. 'I brought a couple of aspirins, too, they can't do any harm.'

'So kind.' Verity looked at them as though she was not too sure of that. She made no attempt to take them. Did she think they might be poison?

'It's getting cold out here.' Nan looked around and shivered. 'Come inside and have a drink before – You *are* staying for dinner?'

'I don't know.' Verity looked to Kingsley.

'You can stay,' he told her. It was not the answer she wanted. 'I'm afraid I must get back to town.'

'You're always so busy.' Nan's tone was just short of scolding. 'You ought to spend an evening here with Lynette. Have dinner with her in her room and play cards afterwards, or just watch television. It would do Lynette a world of good.'

'Lynette . . .' Kingsley sighed deeply. 'You're right, I know. I must organise things so that I can spend more time with her. Perhaps, if she continues to improve, we could take a little trip together, just the two of us –'

'Oh!' Verity's sharp involuntary movement had sent water splashing into her lap. 'Oh!' She leaped to her feet, dropping the glass; more water showered her before the glass hit the grass to roll away unbroken.

'Look at that!' Nan said. 'You can't stay out here now, you'll catch your death of cold. Come inside and we'll find you something dry to wear.'

'Yes . . . No . . .' Verity was trying to brush away the water which was rapidly saturating her skirt.

'All right.' She surrendered ungraciously. Nan took her elbow and urged her firmly towards the house. Verity looked back over her shoulder, obviously unwilling to leave Margot and Kingsley alone together.

But it was Lynette who was her real rival. First Claudia and now Lynette. Verity would never command the whole-hearted devotion she craved, the undivided attention she longed for from Kingsley . . . not while Lynette was alive to come between them.

If Kingsley were to marry Verity, how long would Lynette survive?

'I suppose we ought to go in, too.' Kingsley had risen to his feet, now he turned to Margot.

'Wait!' She had to warn him.

'Yes?' He looked down at her with a trace of impatience. 'What is it?'

Chapter Twenty-One

'. . . Verity,' Margot stammered. 'Verity did it.'

'Did what?'

'Verity,' she said softly but clearly, 'killed that woman.'

'Nonsense!' Kingsley spoke with absolute conviction. 'She couldn't possibly.'

'She did. And . . . and probably Claudia, too.'

'Now just a minute –' Kingsley started to sit down on the bench beside her, then changed his mind. Did he think she might be dangerous, that she might attack him? 'That's a very serious accusation. Verity could sue you for slander. How many people have you told this?'

'No one else. Yet. I've just realised it.'

'Then you'd better unrealise it. I know you've never liked Verity, but that's a terrible thing to say. Why would Verity want to kill anyone?'

'Because Polly Parsons had found out what she was doing and was going to tell you.'

'Oh?' His voice was carefully neutral. 'And just what was Verity doing?'

'She was stealing money from you.'

'Oh? What makes you think that?'

'Verity handled all your travel arrangements – even for your holidays. And she said PoP Tours were very expensive. That was her excuse. They weren't as expensive as she'd like to have you believe. She was inflating the invoices and keeping the difference for herself.'

'No, Margot, no.' He exhaled a long breath before asking curiously, 'And Claudia? Why should she have killed Claudia?'

'Claudia was the first to find out. She confronted Verity and threatened to tell you, perhaps even tell the police. Verity couldn't face that, so . . .' Margot trailed off, she could see Kingsley shaking his head in denial.

'Not plausible, Margot.' Spite and irony struggled for the ascendancy in his voice. 'If that had been the situation, it was far more likely that my late lady, in one of her wild antic moods, would have laughed like a drain – and demanded that Verity split the proceeds with her.'

'Kingsley!'

'Come now, Margot. You knew Claudia. You can't pretend that she was . . . conventional.'

'No . . .' Margot whispered. Conventional was not the word for Claudia. 'But that was why you married her. Because she was different . . . exciting . . . unconventional.'

'Was it? I can hardly remember now.' The spite won, but it was not directed against her. 'Unfortunately, I had no idea just how "different" she was. Or, perhaps more accurately, how different she would grow to be. The years change us all – some more than others. Claudia most of all.'

'Kingsley –'

'I'm only thankful that Lynette doesn't seem to have inherited Claudia's wild streak.'

Wild? Well, yes . . . at moments. More frequent moments as the years went on, Kingsley seemed to be implying. More disturbingly, he was casting new light on what had always seemed to be a perfect marriage.

'Margot –' Kingsley knelt beside her, one hand reaching out to rest lightly on her knee. 'Try to understand –'

Her slight involuntary recoil disturbed Tikki, who

yawned and stretched, his extended claws brushing Kingsley's hand. Kingsley withdrew his hand quickly.

'Margot –' He steadied himself by the armrest of the bench instead. 'I promise you, you're wrong. Verity had nothing to do with all this.'

'I'm afraid I find that rather hard to believe.' Everything fitted together so well – especially the part about Kingsley being too trusting. 'I think we ought to tell the police and let them decide.'

'No, Margot, I can't let you do this to Verity.' Kingsley rose, leaning heavily on the armrest. 'I know none of you have ever liked her, but Verity has been my right arm for many years now. I don't know what I'd have done without her.'

'Even though she killed your wife?'

'Verity did *not* kill Claudia.' Kingsley took a deep unsteady breath. 'I did.'

'What?' Margot was on her feet, too, facing him in the deepening twilight. Dislodged, an indignant Tikki hit the lawn and spat a protest before stalking off.

'I didn't mean to.' There was a hollow note in his voice. *Well, he would say that, wouldn't he?* 'She shocked me so . . . and then she tried to throw herself into my arms, laughing, laughing . . . I just struck out to . . . to push her away. Verity was right: you can forget you have a knife in your hand.'

He didn't seem to have one now. Margot began backing away cautiously.

'No, wait!' He stretched out an imploring hand, but let it fall when she flinched. 'Let me explain –'

'Explain?' Did he really think that was all that was necessary?

'Let me try. Claudia –' His voice broke. 'You knew Claudia. But you didn't know the way she was changing –'

'I hadn't seen her in the past few years.'

'No, you hadn't, but it had been going on for longer than that. Ever since –'

'For God's sake, sit down!' he snapped suddenly.

'I'm all right as I am.' Margot gained another backward step. 'Go on, I'm listening.'

'But are you understanding?' He took a step in her direction. 'No, don't be afraid. I won't hurt you.'

'Oh?' *If he had killed his wife, what chance did she have?* Perhaps Claudia hadn't understood, either. If only her legs felt strong enough to sustain her in a sudden dash to the house – and safety. The garden was too dangerous a place with Kingsley in it.

'Claudia was always . . . erratic. You must admit that. You never knew what she'd do next.'

He had a point there. Margot nodded careful agreement.

'She thrived on excitement, lived for adventure, was . . . was addicted to the adrenaline rush. After that first . . . episode . . . when we were captured and held hostage . . . she became worse . . . more addicted. When we went on subsequent fact-finding missions, she insisted on being taken into the mountains, or the jungle, or wherever "the action" was. She upset our hosts, she worried me, she was beginning to attract the attention of the Foreign Office. I didn't know what to do.'

'Killing her was a bit extreme.' The caustic remark slipped out before Margot could stop it.

'It wasn't necessary . . . then,' he said absently. 'She discovered PoP Tours. I don't know how. Perhaps someone with her . . . tastes . . . told her about them. Perhaps PoP contacted her directly, they seem to have their own ways of knowing who might be interested in what they had to offer.

'I was relieved . . . at first. I even accompanied her in the beginning –' He made a curious sound, half-laugh, half-sob. 'I wanted to make sure she'd be safe on them. After that, she usually went by herself. Verity was right – their tours were a lot more expensive than most, but they were worth it. They kept Claudia happy.'

184

'Nan said Claudia had just come back from the most wonderful tour of her life,' Margot said softly.

'Oh, God!' Kingsley buried his face in his hands. 'You don't know why she had such a wonderful time! Why it was the most thrilling trip of her life!'

'No.' Margot took another step backwards, realising suddenly that she did not want to know.

'You might have guessed. You knew Claudia. When Claudia was happy, it usually meant that she was making someone else miserable.'

'Kingsley!' But the protest was faint. She *had* known Claudia – and too many unpleasant possibilities were suddenly crowding into her mind.

'That last most wonderful trip of her life was the one where Claudia crossed the dividing line. She was no longer content to be an observer, she wanted to be a participant. Not because she believed in any particular cause, not that she gave a damn about any rights or wrongs –' His voice choked with anguish.

'She just wanted to kill!'

'No!' The world began spinning around her. Margot stumbled and fell into the nearest chair. She could not disbelieve him. Too many fragmented memories, disjointed phrases in Claudia's voice, were swirling through her mind.

'*How funny . . . Did you see him jump?*' When Claudia had deliberately aimed the car at the elderly man on the pedestrian crossing, slamming on the brakes at the last possible moment. '*He thought I was actually going to hit him.*' . . . '*Shoplifting? How funny . . . how funny.*' Wild, wild Claudia, growing ever wilder, until . . .

'And she did,' Kingsley went on relentlessly. 'Some poor bloody peasant, a civilian, going about his lawful concerns, trying to dodge the crossfire between opposing factions. He never even noticed Claudia playing sniper. One moment he was there, the next moment he was a heap of rags in the dust. And Claudia had her great big thrill. Now she knew what it felt like to kill.'

185

'So do you,' Margot whispered.

'Not the same,' he refuted indignantly. 'Not the same thing at all. I didn't do it for a thrill . . . it was a necessity.'

'Necessity?'

'Don't you see? She enjoyed it . . . loved it. It was so much fun for her that she was already planning her next trip. She was going to do it again!'

'No!' But she knew he was right. Nan had already told her that. *'Back to the same place . . .'*

'She – she was boasting about it. She couldn't wait to get back there and play sniper some more. She . . . she'd turned into a monster. And she laughed and tried to throw herself into my arms. She thought I'd laugh, too. What did a few poverty-stricken peasants matter? I had to stop her. You do understand, don't you?'

'Yes . . .' she whispered, overwhelmed by the thought of the horror and revulsion Kingsley must have felt as he listened to Claudia's story of her ultimate thrill. No wonder he had lashed out at her unthinkingly – But what was he doing with a knife in his hand in the first place? And also –

'Chloe . . .' The sympathy drained away abruptly. 'How could you have let Chloe take the blame?'

'I didn't mean to, I swear it. I was going to carry Claudia to the car and drive her somewhere . . . where I could leave her. Only Lynette appeared suddenly. She didn't see me; I was in the shadows. She was looking for the cat – he lived here then. She saw her mother, went forward and bent over her. Then Chloe came and saw them both and pulled the knife out. I don't know what happened next. I . . . I blacked out. When I came to, I was back in the London flat. I was in shock, I must have driven back to town on automatic pilot . . .'

'Lynette thought Chloe had killed her mother.' That was a possibility Margot had considered before. 'And Chloe thought Lynette had done it.'

'Time warps at a moment like that. Lynette didn't

186

remember that she got there first. When Chloe pulled out the knife, it must have been such a shock for her that she thought she'd discovered them that way."

'But, when you found yourself in London, you didn't come back to clear Chloe.'

'At first, I thought it was all a nightmare. I'd almost convinced myself of that when they rang from St Albans to tell me the news. I went into shock again . . . had a complete breakdown. The party rushed me into The Priory . . . I don't remember much about that time. When I got out, I found that Chloe was in custody. She wouldn't talk on the phone or answer letters. I began to wonder if Claudia had still been alive when they found her and Chloe *had* killed her – by pulling out the knife. That can happen, you know.'

'Chloe thought she was protecting Lynette.' Margot's sympathy wavered, responding to his need, then falling again as she remembered:

'And what about Polly Parsons?'

'Ah, yes, her.' He sounded as though he had hoped they could forget about her. 'She'd been out of the country at that time. An extended round-the-world tour of global destruction, I believe. She was most upset to get back and learn about Claudia. I think she felt she'd lost one of her best clients. She wanted to discuss . . . taking up the slack, as it were.'

'Blackmail?' Had Polly Parsons lived on the edge of impersonal peril for so long that she had forgotten how much more dangerous the personal could be?

'Oh, she didn't call it that. She just said that she knew how thrilled and delighted Claudia had been with her last trip. She knew why, too. She mentioned writing travel articles for magazines . . . newspapers. I felt she couldn't be trusted. We've had too much experience of chequebook journalism. If the tabloids were to get a whiff of her story –' He shrugged. 'I could never afford to pay her enough to match the sums they could offer.

It would be front page news – and it would drag us all down –'

'So you killed her, too.'

'She tripped and fell.' He was going to stick with that story. 'Perhaps I wasn't quite as quick as I might have been in picking her up – and then it was too late. I was thinking about Lynette . . . about what such a story about her mother might do to her . . .'

'Not about what it might do to your political career?' Henry stepped out of the shadows. He patted Margot's shoulder. 'Good work, you kept him talking. We heard it all.'

'We?'

'It would mean goodbye to that Cabinet post in the next reshuffle.' Emmeline stepped out beside Henry.

They made a formidable pair.

Chapter Twenty-Two

'Don't worry, I'll talk to Comfrey first thing in the morning,' Kingsley assured them. 'He'll be able to work out some sort of discreet arrangement with the authorities.'

Richard and Henry, flanking him as they came out of the study, exchanged glances. Could they trust him?

'Verity can drive me back to town.' Kingsley was trying to give the impression that he still controlled events.

'You'll be all right?' Margot felt compelled to ask, perhaps for old times' sake.

'Eventually . . .' He gave her a wry smile. 'I'll have to have a word with the Prime Minister and tender my resignation as soon as I've talked with Comfrey. Spare the party as much embarrassment as possible, they've had too many scandals in recent years.'

'Scandal?' Verity was quick to pounce. 'What do you mean? What's going on?'

'Nothing. It's all over. I'll explain on the way back to town.' He would have one fully sympathetic listener, at any rate. The discrepancies in his story, already becoming apparent to Margot, would not matter. In Verity's eyes, he could do no wrong.

'Well . . .' Kingsley opened the door and hesitated. Uncle Wilfred nodded. Allowing him a few hours' grace to try to sort out his affairs had been agreed. It would look a lot better if he went to the police of his own accord.

'Tell Lynette . . . Tell Lynette . . .' Kingsley shook his head, looking from one to the other. 'Well, you'll think of something. Just make sure she knows I've always loved her.'

'Kingsley –?' There was a sharp note of anxiety in Verity's voice. 'Kingsley, what –?'

'We must be going now.' He took her arm. 'Come along . . . my darling.'

'Oh!' Verity gasped and looked around to make sure everyone had heard what amounted to a declaration. 'Yes. Yes, my love.'

The door closed behind them.

'I suppose he *will* go back to London?' Richard questioned uneasily. 'They won't go and wrap themselves around a tree, or anything?'

'My money's on a dash for the nearest port,' Henry said. 'A quick trip across to the Continent and then onward to some country we don't have an extradition treaty with. Too bad he killed his best contact for that sort of thing.'

'But the police . . .?' Margot leaned against the wall weakly, although perhaps not as weak as she had been.

'It doesn't matter.' Uncle Wilfred flourished the sheets of paper containing Kingsley's handwritten confession. Whatever happened, Chloe's release was ensured.

'The Prime Minister . . .?'

'It will be in his interests as well as ours to play this down as much as possible,' Richard said.

'It can't be long before there's a plane crash, or natural disaster, or even another scandal.' Emmeline spoke thoughtfully. 'The media will go off chasing that and we'll be forgotten.'

'Really forgotten, this time,' Henry agreed. 'A husband murdering his wife isn't nearly so newsworthy as a twin killing her twin. And with a second woman dead, the whole thing will be presented as some sort of eternal triangle.'

190

Much more palatable than the real truth about Claudia – for all concerned. Memories would fade. Perhaps in another term or two, Emmeline could go back to her school. Aunt Milly would improve with Chloe back home where she belonged. The others could go back to their jobs and take up their lives again.

And Lynette . . .?

Behind them, the stair creaked and they turned to see Lynette slowly and carefully descending, cradling Tikki in her arms. She looked up and became aware of her audience.

'Emmeline took my bell away,' she complained. 'And Tikki's hungry. He wants his dinner.' She glanced uneasily at Uncle Wilfred and added, 'He's going to be a good boy and stay home now. He promised me.'

'He's been spending a lot more time here of late,' Emmeline said. 'Perhaps he *is* back.'

'Perhaps?' Uncle Wilfred gave Tikki an indignant glare. Tikki gave him a melting look in return. He softened. 'Oh, well, give him the benefit of the doubt, eh? Live and let –' Automatically, he broke off, then seemed to realise that such care was no longer necessary. 'Let live!' he finished triumphantly. 'Live and let live!'

'That's the spirit!' Emmeline applauded. 'Just a little while longer and we can all get back to our own lives.'

A little while longer. What a comforting euphemism for *'one last scandal'* – or possibly not, depending on Kingsley's next move. Surely he would try to shield Lynette from any more hurt; wouldn't he?

No one quite dared to remark on Lynette's sudden appearance among them, perhaps afraid that they might startle her into a retreat. It had been a big step for her to take. There were still so many steps to go. So far, so good. Softly . . . softly . . .

Margot closed her eyes briefly and was aware of the comforting pressure of Richard's arm supporting her and Nan's hand patting her shoulder. She opened her eyes and smiled at them. Whatever happened about Kingsley, life would go forward and she had steps of her own to take.

She'd have her good cameras sent on to her from New York. Yes, and she'd keep the apartment there. If the show transferred to Broadway, it would be useful for Christa to have a place to stay. Nor was it likely to be too long before Justin and Fenella got a New York booking. Yes, a family pied-a-terre in Manhattan would be endlessly useful.

'Our Margot has come home,' Uncle Wilfred put an arm around Lynette's shoulders, urging her forward. 'Your Aunt Chloe will be home any day, so why not Tikki, too? Come along, I happen to know there's a very tasty bit of salmon hidden away at the back of the fridge. I was saving it for myself, but –' A beatific smile lit his face. 'I'm not all that hungry somehow. I'll share it with you and Tikki.'